ALL ABOUT US

ALL OR NOTHING SERIES
BOOK ONE

ASHLEY ERIN

*Dedicated to those who are afraid to follow their dreams.
Anything is possible as long as you never give up.*

PROLOGUE

Dane

Pushing the front door open, I sit on the bench just inside the door and pull my cowboy boots off my feet.

"Oh God, that feels so good." Sighing, I contemplate just staying here for the rest of the day. I've been working since sunrise trying to get the north pasture up and running again. The horses are getting restless while we complete the rebuild, and Samson has taken it upon himself to jailbreak the herd out. Damn horse.

My head jerks up and smacks against the wall as a scream and crash sounds from the kitchen.

"Ow." Stalking into the kitchen, rubbing the back of my head, I glare at Lia. "What the hell, Lia? My eardrums almost exploded."

She looks up from where she is picking cutlery off the floor, eyes shining. "Emma is moving home. She called me today and said she is packing up her stuff, selling her place and moving in next door again."

"Cool." Grabbing a glass from the cupboard, I get some water and gulp it down quickly. Emma is coming home? It's been thirteen years since I've seen her, aside from the photos Lia shows us, and in that time a day hasn't gone by that I haven't thought of her.

"Cool? Cool! You have her photo hidden on your dresser and all you have to say is COOL?" Lia gapes at me and I shrug, smirking at her.

"Gotta go take a shower." I back out of the kitchen, chuckling at Lia's growl of frustration. She's so easy to rile up.

Taking the steps two at a time, I shut my bathroom door and turn on the water before stepping into my bedroom to strip off my clothes. Emma's picture peeks out at me from its place on my dresser and I pick it up, heart pounding.

Emma's mom came into their kitchen from checking on Emma. She smiled at me before pouring me a cup of juice.

"She's fine, Dane, falls happen when you work with horses." Mr. Hayle planted his hand on my shoulder, trying to make me feel better about her getting bucked off the horse I told her to ride. I though he was safe and I was wrong.

Instead of accepting his comfort, I looked at Emma's parents and decided to tell them.

"One day, I'm going to marry Emma, Mr. and Mrs. Hayle, and I promise I will do my best to make sure she never gets hurt."

They looked at each other and smiled, before turning to listen as I said, "I love Emma. I won't fail again."

"Dane, love isn't preventing the hurt, it's being there during the hurt." She scooched closer to me, taking her napkin and wiped the smudge of dirt off my face.

I didn't care what she said. I loved her and I was going to protect her.

Emma is coming home. A grin stretches out on my face; finally, I can make her mine.

CHAPTER ONE

Dane

Peering out of the window, my hands find their way into my hair when there is still no sign of Emma. Giggling catches my ear and I turn to glare at Lia. She slaps her hand over her mouth and leaves the room, bursts of laughter echoing throughout the house. Dammit. She is going to be hard to live with now.

People don't think it's possible for an eleven-year-old boy's heart to break, but when Emma and her parents moved away thirteen years ago, my heart shattered. That was the girl I was going to marry and they took her away. Realistically, I know she isn't the same girl she once was, but no one has ever measured up to my memories of her and now I have a chance. A chance at what I always thought would be.

I never connected with her on Facebook, simply because the realist in me doesn't want to see if she's not the person I've built in my mind. I don't consider myself a romantic, but

Emma was the girl next door. She was my friend and then one day I realized I thought she was cool for a girl. I fell for her at a young age and my heart has clung to that love ever since.

Glancing at the clock, I groan. The minutes are passing slowly and yet it's somehow already time to do chores. Today has been the longest fucking day ever.

I'm in my office placing yet another lumber order when Lia comes bouncing in the door with a big grin on her face.

"What's up, crazy face?" She seriously looks manic and it's a little unsettling. I return my focus to the order form on the screen in front of me. We've had several severe wind storms and the number of broken fences is stacking up faster than we can fix them. It may be time to hire some help, but I don't have time to screen applicants.

"Oh nothing . . . I just know something you don't." She drops into the seat across from me and waves her hand in front of my screen, smirking at me. I roll my eyes at her before knocking her hand away so I can close out the order and submit it.

"Don't all women feel that they know something all men don't?" I ask while checking my email to ensure I received the confirmation of my order before closing out the web browser. Leaning back in my chair, hands clasped behind my head, I arch my brow at her. Lia hates that I can arch my brow when she can't and the glare she shoots my way makes me smirk.

"We do. But in this case, it's something that you desperately want to know." She pauses emphatically and I silently wait, not feeding in to her dramatics. "Okay fine. I will tell you. You're ruining my fun."

"You always did have the patience of a toddler." Smirking

at her as she sticks her tongue out at me, I refrain from doing the same to her.

"I just thought that you might like to know about the truck and trailer that just pulled up outside. A certain brunette is currently unloading her horses and I know that you've been resisting plastering your face to the window waiting for her. It's hilarious seeing you this way, big brother." Her eyes sparkle at me as I resist the urge to leap out of my chair.

With forced casualness, I remain in my seat. "Good to know. Are you going over to say hi?" *Please say no. Oh, please say no.*

Lia's eyes narrow at me and disappointment flashes in them briefly as she searches my face before a smug smile settles on her lips. "Nope. I would love to, but I need to go to complete two treatment schedules for some new clients." She pauses as she stands and starts to head out the door. Stopping, she looks back at me. "She looks like hell, Dane. We FaceTimed earlier today and you can hardly recognize her. I just want you to be prepared for when you see her." She leaves and I wait until I hear the back door slam before rushing upstairs and outside.

∼

Emma

Exhaling in relief at the fact that the long journey I have undertaken is almost over, I glance at my GPS to see how far I have left to go. In about five more kilometers I need to start looking for the mailboxes, it's sad to me that I don't know this way by heart, but Grandpa always came to visit us after my last visit.

Gazing at the scenery around me, taking in the rolling hills mixed with prairie and woods, I feel a sense of peace that has evaded me in over ten months. I love the mixture of landscapes, and searching for wildlife along the way keeps the drive interesting. The lone hawk swooping in the clear blue sky or the fox watching for gophers has me distracted from all the other thoughts I am avoiding.

It has been seven years since I was last at my grandfather's acreage. *I guess I need to refer to it as my acreage now.* My eyes well with tears as I think of the circumstances bringing me back after all this time. I haven't really confronted the series of events leading me to this moment. I'm not ready.

Shaking my head, I refocus on the sun shining and the expanse of endless blue sky instead of going to that sad place I'm actively pretending doesn't exist. I've become an expert at pretending. People don't like to look below the surface. They don't like to get to the root of someone, it's easier to just accept what others show you.

Slowing my truck to avoid missing my turn so I don't have to turn around with the horse trailer, I think I finally see them at the top of the next hill. Sure enough, as I get closer there are two mailboxes next to a long and winding driveway.

The first, as I expect, says Hyatt, for my neighbors and old family friends. The second, I'm surprised, says Hayle instead of Ellis as I was anticipating. I guess when I told Lia I was moving up she decided to change it for me. I cannot wait to see my oldest and dearest friend. We have remained close despite not seeing each other for seven years, an accomplishment if you ask me.

Breathing a sigh of relief as I turn into the tree lined driveway, the stress from the drive slowly starts to lift. Ever since my parents died in a car accident nine and a half months ago, being in a vehicle always causes me anxiety.

Driving is stressful, being a passenger borders on the impossible.

I scan the winding driveway with a sense of nostalgia and repress any thoughts of my weaknesses. The shade from the trees provides reprieve from the sweltering heat of this unseasonably warm Alberta June so I release my hair from the confines of the messy bun I had haphazardly mounded it into. I prefer to wear it down unless I'm working, but even with my air conditioning it was too hot in the sun to leave it down.

The rays of the sun shimmer through the trees making the driveway seem almost magical, although in my opinion the raw land surrounding us is magical and I hope being back here will work that magic on me. Fix me. Heal me. Take away the pain.

Shaking my head, I return my thoughts to the surroundings outside. The houses are a short drive down the winding driveway, lined with lush, thick brush and trees, providing privacy from the road. This is one of the things I love most about these properties, the privacy.

My new, err old, home is situated inside the Hyatt's sprawling 320-acre ranch. I have ten blissful acres to call my own and I eagerly watch for the first glimpse in seven years of my childhood home.

The trees start to thin, giving me fleeting glimpses of the expansive yard holding both my house and the Hyatt's. My home, a Victorian style house is on the west side of the road, while the Hyatt's ranch style home is on the east side directly across from mine. I had lived with my parents and my grandfather on this property until my dad's job relocated us when I was ten years old. I have not been back to visit since I was sixteen years old.

Grandpa had renovated the Victorian style home five years ago and the photos he had sent me did not do it justice. The house is a soft yellow with a wraparound covered porch, complete with a porch swing, turret, and a bright blue door. The porch swing is calling my name but it's going to have to wait. It will be the perfect place to work on my next novel or to curl up with a good book.

Moving my gaze to the well-kept horse corrals, I'm thankful that they have been maintained. Knowing that the Hyatts have put in effort to upkeep the property brings back memories of all the good times I shared with Lia, Dane, and Ryan, and the devastation I felt getting into the truck and driving away from them.

Tears ran down my cheeks, leaving silent tracks of pain as I watched Mom and Dad close up the moving van. Lia's arm snaked around my waist as we watched Aunty Juliette and Uncle Darren say their goodbyes.

My eyes blurry as I ran into the barn, ignoring Mom's shout of protest. Racing to the back stall, I opened it up and closed myself in with Whisper. She's laying down, so I crawled onto her back and buried my face into her mane. Muffled voices drifted into the barn, but I ignored them.

"Emma?" Wiping my eyes, I looked up at Ryan. He slid open the stall door and came to sit next to me. "They're waiting for you."

Shaking my head, I wiped my cheeks with a roughness that caused Ryan to drag my hands away from my face. "Stop hurting yourself. Em, it sucks, but we can't change anything. Remember, no matter where you live we all love you and that will never change."

"I'm scared." He pulled me up and hugged me. Ryan acted like my big brother. Until that moment, I'd always hated it, but knowing I wouldn't have his brotherly presence anymore makes me wish I had appreciated it more.

"I know." He released me, pulling me out of the stall and picking up his pitchfork. "Goodbye, Em."

I dragged my feet as I left the barn, my heart pounding as I stared at the moving van in resentment. Lia and Dane stood side by side, watching me. Lia was crying, Dane's fists clenched at his side.

When Mom tried to wrap her arm around me, I jumped away, rushing into Lia's arms. She whispered to me, her words falling on deaf ears. Stepping back, I ducked my head under Dane's chin and hugged him.

"I wish you weren't leaving." His voice choked. Looking up, I saw the shimmer of withheld tears. "I'm going to miss you."

"I'm going to miss you all too." Dad rested his hands on my shoulders, pulling me away firmly but gently. In my heart, I knew this is hard on them too, but I yanked myself away and jumped into the back of the truck, slamming the door behind me.

Mom and Dad got in and started the truck. Staring out the window, fresh tears fell as I watched Dane and Lia chasing us. Lia fell behind, but Dane kept running until I could no longer see him in the cloud of dust from the dirt road. His face, distorted in agony is the only thing I saw as we turned away from the only home I've ever known.

Pulling up to the house alongside a small paddock, I gratefully hop out of the truck and open the back door to let Chloe out.

Chloe is a gorgeous three-year-old Doberman Pinscher that I adopted as a puppy from a rescue specifically for misunderstood breeds and I'm grateful every day to have her. She is completely dedicated to me and especially in the past year I have desperately needed her comforting presence.

Chloe stretches and bumps my hand with her nose to get a head scratch before taking off to explore her new home. Grinning as she takes in all the new scents while keeping within eyesight of me, I walk to the back of the horse trailer and unlatch the door, smiling at the happy whinnies that greet me.

My two horses, Serenity and Belle, have been wonderful during the long trek and I want to get them settled with some hay and water before unpacking the belongings I have in my trailer.

Climbing into the trailer, I unhook Serenity and lead her across the lawn to the fence. Grabbing some brushes from the tack compartment, I give her a quick rub down. She is one of the gentlest, kindest, and most stunning horses I have ever seen.

Serenity is a dusty buckskin mare and her unique coloring always draws attention. While most people think of her as brown, her coat almost has a bronze tinge to it. The stark black of her mane and tail set off the color so she really shines.

Hopping back into the trailer, I lead out Belle and brush her quickly as well. Belle is my curvaceous beauty, a ridgeback dun with the sweetest personality. She is quiet and calm. My third horse, a bay named Chandler, won't be arriving until my best friend Alex arrives sometime in July. Chandler had a limp when I went to load him and I didn't want to risk the drive so Alex agreed to look after him.

Gathering their leads, I walk into the pen closest to the house. I want to keep a watchful eye until I know they are settled to their new environment. Removing their halters and lead ropes I grin as they both find a patch of dirt and roll. While they are rolling and getting acquainted with their new home, I take the time to stretch out my sore muscles and gaze around me.

My little acreage has the perfect mixture of rolling hills and flat prairie with a small forest that takes up about half of the property. There are riding trails throughout and I can't wait to explore it in its entirety once I have unpacked.

Whistling for Serenity and Belle before taking off at a quick jog, they join up with me as we do our customary run. It feels amazing after being cooped up in the truck for the past 12 hours.

I begin walking backwards so I can check how my girls are moving, not paying attention to my surroundings. It's too late for my balance when I feel a ridge behind my knees and I'm falling, quickly submerged into the full water trough I hadn't noticed by the fence.

"Shit!" I holler, sputtering as I try to push my hair out of my face and crawl out of the water at the same time.

Rough hands grip my arms, pulling me out as I yelp in surprise. A deep, masculine laugh fills me with horror and embarrassment.

Oh no . . .

As I'm set on the ground, the hands falling away once I'm steady, I shiver.

"I guess that's one way to cool down." The low, amused voice sends tingles down my spine.

Pushing my soaking hair out of my face and closing my eyes to gather my wits, I take a deep breath before looking up at my rescuer. My brain freezes as I stare at Dane in shock and embarrassment.

Oh. My. God.

The burning of my face betrays me as a blush spreads over my cheeks and I resist burying my face into my hands. Dane chuckles and slowly moves his gaze over me, starting at my sandaled feet and making his way up my bare legs to my soaked yoga shorts and tank top.

I can feel it clinging to me and the cool breeze causing my nipples to stand at attention, like this moment wasn't already humiliating enough. Fuck my life.

Lastly, he examines my flushed face, the mess that is my wet and tangled hair and settles on my green eyes with a sexy grin.

Trying to maintain some dignity, I arch a brow at the humored expression in his gaze and decide to return the favor.

I haven't seen Dane since he was eleven years old and at twenty-four, he has become a devastatingly handsome man. His jeans and shirt accentuate his strong, well-toned muscles. He is tall and I need to tilt my head back slightly to examine his face. His strong and chiseled jaw, short, perfectly styled hair, and pale green eyes complete the swoon worthy package.

He was cute as a boy, but the man in front of me has ignited my hormones as my mind wanders to all the dirty things I could do to him, starting with those kissable lips. This train of thought makes me blush even darker and I quickly move my eyes away from his lips to his eyes.

His shocked expression at my boldness is apparent at the drop in his jaw and I smirk at him cheekily. This past year has changed me into a shell of who I was, but I'm not the shy ten-year-old he once knew, the one who followed him around doing whatever he wanted just to spend time with him.

Thirteen years have passed since I last saw Dane and his brother Ryan. They were both away working when I visited last. Their sister, Lia, has been my best friend since before we understood what a friend was. This family was once a huge part of my life, I'm hoping that connection still remains.

Finally feeling a little more composed, considering the circumstances, I grin at him mischievously and before he can stop me, I step in and give him a hug. My heart kicks up a notch when his hard muscles press against me, I can't help my mind from wandering straight back into the gutter.

Stepping back quickly I smirk at the water now soaking his front before the hard ridges of his abs molding to his shirt distracts me. Dragging my gaze away from the delectable muscles teasing me, I check to make sure I haven't physically started to drool.

The thrumming of my body reacting to his has me squirming as I try to refocus my thoughts away from imagining what it would be like to run my hands over his stomach and . . .

What the fuck is wrong with me? This is Dane. We used to go on adventures in the forest and have movie nights in their rec room. What is it about this reunion that has shifted him from friend to a man my heart flutters over? Blushing at the humiliating entrance back into his life and the line my thoughts are crossing, I search for the first thing I can think of to say.

"Where are Lia and Ryan?" I must be imagining the disappointment that flashes across his face at the abrupt shift. There is no way he could be thinking along the same lines as me, I know how awful I look. The shadows under my eyes, the heaviness I now carry with me, I hardly recognize myself when I look in the mirror.

"Lia had some work she needed to get done for new clients and Ryan is checking the south fence line. I came to invite you over for dinner at Lia's request." He smirks at me as I stand soaking wet in front of him. "Dinner is at six, so you have time to—compose yourself."

Ignoring his banter, I gratefully accept the invitation as I did not stop along the way to pick up any supplies. With one last chuckle and a look I can't decipher he saunters away from me. My eyes seem to be glued to him as he walks away, his jeans snugly forming to his perfect ass. Mentally shaking myself I peel my eyes away before turning to the house.

CHAPTER TWO

Dane

"Lia!" Shutting the door behind me, I yell for her as I head to the freezer. "You invited Emma over for dinner!" Peering in, I grab some steaks and turn around ready to yell some more. Lia stands behind me, grinning when I jump at her proximity. "Fuck! Way to be a creeper."

She takes the steaks from my hands, setting them on the counter.

"Not that I wasn't planning on inviting her, but it's sweet that you read my mind." She mocks me, so I give her a gentle shove. Grabbing an apple from the basket on the counter, I wink at her and head to my room. She drives me insane, but I know her heart is in the right place.

Collapsing onto my bed I finally allow myself to think about Emma. Up close and personal. When I saw her running with her horses, my heart swelled at the ease and beauty before me. Seeing her dripping wet, standing in front of me—

her wet tank top hugging her glorious curves made me instantly erect and straining in my jeans.

Emma is a stunning woman and I wanted nothing more than to pull her into my arms. My dick is hardening in my jeans as I think of her and I adjust myself, groaning when I think about how she pressed her body into mine. It's clear my body finds her attractive, and the bit of spunk she showed me was intriguing. All the qualities I remember from childhood seem to have strengthened and grown.

How should I go about pursuing her? We hardly know each other anymore. She is obviously physically attracted to me, her pert nipples saluting me and the soft intake of breath when we hugged were a dead giveaway.

Her green eyes are brighter than I remember yet tinged with sadness. The loss she has suffered this year has been great and it pisses me off that I missed the funerals. Yet, I was still shocked to see the depth of the sadness and a trace of guardedness that was unexpected, especially turned on me. Add to that the deep purple shadows under her eyes and how thin she is, I want to wrap her in my arms and guard her from further hurt. Lia tried to prepare me, but nothing could have equipped me for the physical toll the past year has taken on her body and mind.

I'm conflicted with what to do. My body tells me to rush the process, my heart tells me to show her how I feel, and my mind tells me to let her get settled, find some calm and then gauge where she is at. At war with myself, I know my body will lose. Only time can heal the wounds she has and I need to be patient.

I'm not patient.

It's against my nature, but I won't push her. As challenging as it will be to deny fulfilling the dream I've held onto since childhood, I want her to be ready because I have been ready for years. Regardless of letting her settle in and having time to heal, there is no harm in flirting . . . Right?

Rolling off my bed, I look out my window and at her house. *What is going through your mind as you walk through there?* My legs ache to go see how she is doing, instead I shoot Ryan a text to find out where he is. I need a distraction.

"Emma's here and settling in. She's coming for dinner later." Dismounting Charger, I walk over to where Ryan is trimming Eore's hooves.

Ryan finishes up, handing me Eore's lead rope as he packs up his tools. "Awesome. How is she?"

He knows how I feel about her, but, unlike Lia, he doesn't say much. He just wants everyone to be happy and will do whatever he can to make it happen.

"She fell in a water trough because she wasn't watching where she was going." I close the gate behind Eore and hang his halter and lead rope on it.

"Seriously?" Ryan shakes his head, smirking.

Laughing, I nod but quickly sober as I fill him in on how she really looked.

"It was awful to see how this whole situation has impacted her. They were always so close and it looks like the weight of the world is on her shoulders."

Ryan purses his lips and halters Odin before handing me the lead rope and picking up the first foot. "I can't even imagine being in her shoes. We all squeezed Mom and Dad a little harder after the accident. Then to follow that with Will's heart attack . . . We would be a wreck too."

Nodding in agreement, my thoughts swirl over ways I can make things better.

"Dane, you can't fix this. You know that. It takes time." Ryan gives me a pointed look, already knowing where my thoughts have gone.

"Fuck, I know. Why do you have to know me so damn well? I hate that you always tell me how it is. Can't you lie once in a while?" Looking around the pasture, I notice a rail is down. Grateful for the distraction, I return my attention to Ryan. "When you're done I have a rail to fix. I'm going to check this entire pasture; these wind storms are killing me."

"Just go. I do this by myself all the time." He waves me off so I drop the lead and pull myself onto my saddle.

~

Moaning as my back cracks, I stretch and admire my handiwork. A few rails were busted but the pen is secure again. Checking the weather forecast, I sigh in relief that there doesn't seem to be anymore storms in our near future.

My phone dings with a text just as I finish packing my drill and screws into the saddlebags resting over Chandler's hindquarters.

Lia: Supper is in half hour. You better damn well be ready!

Chuckling to myself, I swing up onto Charger's saddle and take off at a canter. With the distraction of fixing the fence gone, my mind is drawn right back to Emma.

It's time to put some light back into her eyes.

~

Emma

. . .

Standing in the foyer of my new home, the reality of my solitude finally sinks in and I collapse onto one of the boxes piled in the foyer, gazing around me. Tears stream down my face as I take in the photos lining the stairs directly to my right.

Photos of me with my parents, grandfather, and the Hyatts look down at me. Between settling the estate of my parents, followed quickly by that of my grandfather, I have lost my entire family in one fell swoop. All that I have been holding in explodes to the surface like a geyser. Taking deep breaths to push off the anxiety I feel roaring through my head, I stand and dry myself off with a towel I manage to dig out of some boxes. Tossing it onto a box, I close my eyes and attempt to settle my nerves.

Instead of exploring the house right away, I finish unloading the boxes from the trailer. By the time I'm done, the foyer is full, aside from a narrow path leading through them.

Kicking off my shoes, I abandon them to finally check out my childhood home.

Wandering through the house with tears flowing freely down my face, the beauty of what Grandpa has done with me in mind, astounds me. The tile floors, soft green walls, and large windows make this house bright and airy. Grandpa put in a library for me knowing I would one day inherit this home. He even added an amazing writing desk for in the winters when I cannot sit outside to work on my novels.

The kitchen has updated granite countertops and looks into the family room. It is obvious that Grandpa had me in mind with the cozy furniture and space for even more books. Sitting on the couch, I wipe my eyes and pull myself together. I will not allow myself to wallow as it does not change anything. Taking a final glance around the main floor I head back to the pile of boxes and start carrying them to the rooms they belong in. This is a new chapter and I am going to make the most of it.

It does not take me long to get organized, I was meticulous when packing and loading my trailer, which I'm grateful for because it could have been a tedious task.

I made sure my office necessities and books were the first thing I unloaded, I know where my priorities lie. Other than my books, my clothes and other personal items, I had sold everything else prior to moving. The home had been decorated with me in mind and I love seeing Grandpa's personal touch throughout the house.

Every nook and cranny of the house fits my style, he hit it on the nose right down to the little knick-knacks scattered throughout. The layout is open and airy, perfectly laid out for convenience, right down to the enormous walk-in closet that I currently stand in. I'm pretty sure I'm in shock at how large and organized it is. He even put in a wall of shelves for my shoes. This closet is every woman's dream and I can't help but squeal quietly to myself.

The upstairs has three bedrooms, but two will go to Alex once he comes up here. Alex has been my best friend since I was twelve years old and we are inseparable. He is two years older than me and basically my big brother.

Alex automatically agreed to come with me once he knew I was serious about moving, there was no hesitation for him to relocate and I'm eager for him to arrive in the next month or so.

He was basically adopted into our family after his father left them and his mother turned to substances rather than being strong for her son. He is the only family I have left, aside from the Hyatts.

Thinking of Alex reminds me that I need to call him, he will be expecting me to let him know I've arrived safe. Chewing on my lip, I debate whether to call now or later, but unpacking my meagre belongings before dinner wins out, especially since I know he will sense the sorrow I'm purposefully ignoring. I will call him before I head over to see Lia, Dane, and Ryan.

Busying myself with getting settled, I start in my office. This room will contain the most important things to me. It is my life. Everything I need for my writing is contained in the boxes before me, but I want to unpack my books first.

The first box I open has me tearing up again as I pull out the books stacked on top. They are mine and not just any books, but the ones I signed and gave to my mom whenever they came out.

Mom was my biggest fan and had encouraged me in my dream to write, which is why my first novel was published before I turned twenty-one. She helped me in every way she could, including researching every aspect of publishing so I could put all my energy into writing. She was my cheerleader, my beta reader, and my motivator. Returning my focus to the books before me, I place them on the shelf closest to my desk, fingers gliding over them lovingly before quickly unpacking the rest of my boxes.

As usual, I lose track of time in my world of books and putting my favorites in esteemed places that by the time I check the clock I have forty-five minutes to get ready for dinner. Letting Chloe in from her exploration outside, I feed her before hopping in the shower.

Instead of rushing through my shower, I take time to allow the hot water to ease the tension from my neck and shoulders as I mentally make a to-do list for the next few days. Drying off, I wander into my closet to find something to wear.

Flipping through the hangers, I pull out a turquoise halter styled sundress. Considering my re-entrance back into Dane's life, I'm hoping to make an impression at dinner. Instead of examining why I care so much, I try to focus on seeing Ryan and Lia. Will things flow back to the way they once were?

Obviously with Dane things may be a little different. . . my mind wanders back to my encounter Dane and just thinking of him has my heart beating a little faster.

It does not bode well that I have spent five minutes with the man and already developed a crush on him. I need to nip that in the bud, it can't happen. We are neighbors and practically family; aside from my obvious issues, I don't need to add another complexity to my life. They are too close and the situation is too complex. Not to mention my recent dating history has left nothing to be desired. Ugh, I cannot go there right now!

I blow dry my long hair so it hangs in waves down my back, sitting just above my hips. My makeup is soft and natural, completing my look. It may be silly but I want to look good without appearing to try too hard. Why does being a woman have to be so difficult? I'm pretty sure Dane can roll out of bed and still be drop-dead gorgeous.

Examining myself in the mirror, I'm satisfied with what I see. Before heading downstairs, I sweep my hair aside to look at the new tattoo on my back. The intricate design goes straight down my spine in loops and curlicues with three hearts for both of my parents and my grandfather. I will never tire of looking at it.

Grabbing my phone, I stop to scratch Chloe on the head before stepping onto my porch. I gaze around my property, the sun warm on my skin. I love the view of green grass, tall trees, and seeing my horses graze contentedly in their corral.

Breathing in the fresh air, I feel it in my soul that what I need is here. This is where I will heal, while staying connected with what I have lost. Checking on the horses quickly, I toss them some more hay before walking to the Hyatt's. Their parents now live on the back forty of the property, leaving the main house to Lia, Dane, and Ryan. I can't wait to reconnect with the entire family.

Barely stepping into the house, a blur of dark brown hair, brown eyes, and white teeth tackles me at the door. Hugging Lia as we stumble, laughing at the fact that the only reason we're still standing is because she has pushed me up against the door.

"I am so glad you're finally here!" Lia squeals.

"Obviously, you're practically feeling me up. At least romance me first." Chuckling I look over as Ryan comes into the room and laughs at Lia plastering me against the wall.

"That's one way to welcome Emma back into our lives."

Lia releases me from her iron clad grip and I move to stand next to Ryan. He is slightly taller than Dane and I have to crane my neck to look up at him. His dark brown hair is tousled from him running his hands through it. Ryan's rich brown eyes twinkle at me and his smile automatically has my lips twitching in response.

"Hey, squirt," he says affectionately, "it's good to have you back, despite the circumstances that brought you here." Leaning in for one of his bear hugs, I blink back more tears trying to fight their way through. What the hell is wrong with me? I haven't allowed myself to get so emotional after I realized it made people uncomfortable. Despite my show of emotion his hug is soothing and I relax into his embrace.

Pulling away I can't help but notice that I didn't react to him like I did Dane despite the fact that he is equally attractive. He is more rugged than Dane, with a five o'clock shadow on his defined jawline and a roughness that is hard to describe, yet there is no physical reaction to him.

Ryan is the eldest of the three at twenty-eight and was always the one I went to when I needed comfort and a big brother. Lia and Dane were the two I got into mischief with.

When push comes to shove though, even after all these years, I know I can count on any one of them for anything. Glancing around I can't help noticing there is no sign of Dane and try to tamp down the feeling of disappointment.

Looking back at Ryan I realize he is waiting for me to say something. "It feels right to be here, this is where I feel a connection to all of them, even though it's been a bit emotional." Taking a deep breath, I try not to dwell on how much I miss them. It does feel right to be here, but the hole their loss has created still gapes wide open.

"Well, you know we're here for you," he says with a squeeze.

"Can I help with dinner?" Changing the subject away from the one topic I tend to avoid, I look for an escape. I'm not good with talking about this subject matter and want dinner to be lighthearted. I need it to be lighthearted.

"No! You sit and relax, I'm almost ready." Lia leads me into the kitchen and pours me a glass of wine. Gazing around the familiar kitchen taking in its red walls with white cupboards and gleaming granite countertops, it doesn't feel like any time has passed. The stainless steel appliances are new, but it still feels like a second home. Moving towards the center island, I sit at the breakfast bar setting my phone on the counter. Cradling the glass set in front of me, I sip my wine.

"Where is Dane?" Inquiring in what I hope is a casual tone of voice; I gaze at Lia and take another sip of my wine. I know if I don't make eye contact with her she will find it suspicious and I curse the burn of a blush forming in my cheeks.

"He was running behind this afternoon and is washing up," Ryan replies as he steps inside from lighting the barbeque. He looks at me closely before observing, "I can't believe how much you've changed. You're no longer a little squirt."

Laughing at his scrutiny I reply, "Well, that's what thirteen years does to a person. Although, compared to you I'm still a squirt." Considering that Ryan and Dane are both taller than I am but also strong and muscled, I am tiny compared to them. Both men are built from all the work done on the ranch and have the muscles to show for it. Ryan and Dane are natural protectors of those they care about. One time in the first grade, a bully had tripped me and I flew face first into the sand. Ryan saw and gave him a black eye. Looking at Ryan now, I still see that intensely devoted man and grin at him.

He winks at me, grabbing the plate of steaks and heading back outside to put them on the grill.

"Lia, are you sure I can't help?"

"You've already had a long enough day and supper is ready once the steaks are done." She starts to load food onto the table and I get up to help her, ignoring the mock glare she shoots in my direction. As I carry the salad over to the table I look hungrily at the mountain of food she has begun piling there, my stomach loudly growls causing Lia and me to burst out laughing. The realization that I haven't eaten since breakfast has me distracted as I drool over the feast Lia has put together, more embarrassingly audible growls coming from my midsection and I don't notice Dane walk into the room.

"Hey, Emma, acquaint yourself with any more water troughs this afternoon?" I swivel around to glare at him, barely resisting sticking my tongue out as Ryan and Lia start laughing.

"Once was enough, but thanks for checking," I mutter as my face turns an embarrassing shade of red. Meeting Dane's eyes, I notice that his brows are furrowed and his eyes are studying me closely. I squirm under his scrutiny, not sure what he is thinking. If it was Alex, I could read his thoughts just by his expression, but I don't know Dane well enough anymore and his expression causes heat to spread through me.

"What?" I finally ask after a moment, giving him my sassiest look. Somewhere inside me the girl with confidence is hiding and I draw upon her to deal with the rush of emotions Dane causes to course through me.

He smirks at me. "I was jus—"

The sound of my cell ringing cuts him off. Dane reaches over and grabs my phone, glancing at the screen before passing it to me with a look. I glance down and see Alex's name on the screen.

"Shit . . ." Ignoring the curious looks from my friends, I swipe the screen. "I am so so SO sorry!"

"Holy shit, Em! What the hell? You're gone for not even a day and already forgetting me? I was worried sick! I know how driving is for you and it was a long journey. Did your trip go okay?" Alex's voice is clearly audible throughout the silence in the kitchen so I meander over to the window to try to get some distance. Quickly turning down the volume before I reply.

I don't miss the way Dane is watching me closely as I turn my body fully away from him. "I know. I can't believe I forgot. The drive was okay, better than we thought it would be. I got distracted after letting the horses out. I decided to take a bath in the water trough." I chuckle as he bursts out laughing. Feeling my face flush again I glance discreetly at Dane. He is still studying me with that unreadable expression, but there is a twitch to his lips as he sees me looking at him. Tuning back into what Alex is saying, I close my eyes listening to the steadying sound of his voice.

"Only you."

"Yep, to add insult to injury I had an audience as Dane had come down to invite me for dinner." I purposely keep my back turned to my captive audience as his laughter comes over the phone. "Hey, can I call you later? I'm just visiting now."

"Yeah, sure. Make sure you actually call me. It's going to be awhile before I can finish making my arrangements and make it up there. I miss you."

"I miss you too. Love you and talk to you later." Hanging up I turn back to my friends and smile sheepishly. Lia looks at me and I mouth, "Alex" to her. She nods in understanding before gesturing to the table.

Lia has everything ready for dinner and we sit at the table as Ryan sets the steaks down. My heart flutters when I see Dane looking at me contemplatively.

I've known Dane since we were children and never reacted this way. Granted, I was ten the last time I saw him. Looking at him from under my lashes, I can't help but get caught up in how utterly gorgeous he is. He could have anyone he wanted and even if he wanted me, the last thing I need is to complicate this relationship, especially since I live within sight of his home. I just need to keep reminding myself of that.

Dinner is spent catching up with each other. Ryan has his own farrier business that he runs out of Lia's clinic where she does massage therapy on horses. Dane has focused entirely on the running of the property and feels passionately about their land. They all train horses and Lia competes in reining competitions. I am fascinated hearing about all they have been up to over the years. My ears perk up when we start discussing relationships.

"Ryan and Dane are eternally single." Lia grins at me with a wink. "Dane even has this ridiculous three date rule. Although, I was glad for it with Yvette . . ." Lia makes a face at me that tells me just what she thought of Yvette. "I, on the other hand, am not opposed to a relationship, but men seem to be put off by my drive and supreme awesomeness." I laugh at Lia's sassy outlook on her lack of a relationship, but I know that there is pain behind her words.

"Hey! Don't judge my three date rule! It's come in handy,

as you just pointed out!" Dane protests with a grin. Ryan just sits there and rolls his eyes. I can tell this is an ongoing joke they have and I can't help but laugh and tease along with everyone.

"What about you? How's work? Do you have anyone special in your life?" Ryan asks. I quickly fill them in on taking a bit of a hiatus from writing in order to get settled here before writing the final book in my current series.

Blushing I skip over the boyfriend subject muttering, "There is not much to share on the boyfriend front that would be of interest to you. No one really special to speak of." What I don't say is that I don't seem to have much luck with guys these days. The last guy I was seeing couldn't handle being around me after my parents died and that fizzled out. Since then I haven't bothered too much. I have dealt with it and feel better off immersing myself into my writing rather than focusing on meeting men.

I've been visiting with my friends for over three hours when I stand and ask them to excuse me. "It's been a long day and I'm ready to crash."

"Of course, why don't you come for breakfast tomorrow and we can make plans. I've taken a few days off so I can help out if you need me." Lia gives me a hug as we walk to the door. I wave at Ryan and Dane before closing the door.

Walking slowly back to my house, I tilt my head back so I can gaze at the clear evening sky. The sky is that gorgeous mixture of colors of the setting sun and I decide to sit on my porch instead of going inside so I can enjoy the oranges, pinks, and reds. I want to enjoy the view while I call Alex back. Glancing back to the house across the way as I dial Alex, I stare as I meet Dane's eyes briefly before he turns and goes back inside.

"Hey," he greets me as I let Chloe out of the house before

sitting on the porch swing. She takes off sniffing and I sigh a real sigh of contentment.

"I'm sorry again about not calling. After my little incident and the overwhelming emotions from the house it totally slipped my mind."

"You mean you buried yourself into the practical work of unpacking rather than let yourself be sad," he clarified for me.

I smile to myself. No one knows me better than Alex so I don't bother denying it. "It was nice seeing my old friends again. It's like we picked up right where we left off." I filled him in on Lia's holistic practice, Ryan's farrier business, and how Dane is running the ranch with Ryan's help. They have been breeding Quarter Horses for several generations and have a strong reputation in the community.

"I still can't believe that my first time seeing Dane in thirteen years and he witnesses me falling into a water trough. How humiliating." I typically don't let things embarrass me too badly and laugh stuff off, but for some reason this one has climbed the humiliation mountain to stake its claim. It's difficult not to dwell on that, and I've decided to embrace my need to have a girly moment.

Alex chuckles, "Would you have been so embarrassed if it was Lia or Ryan?"

"O—of course!" I stutter.

"Mmmm hmmm." He doesn't believe me, but lets my lie slide. There is a smile in his voice as he updates me on what he did since he saw me off this morning.

"Chandler's leg seems to be better so he should be ready to go when I am. My packing is coming along and the condo has successfully been sold, they take possession in a few weeks. I figure I should be arriving in about a month. Three weeks if everything flows smoothly." That puts his arrival into the end of June, first week of July.

"I hope you arrive sooner. I miss you, and Chandler," I reply on a yawn.

We chat for a while longer as I describe the house and skirt over the rush of emotions being here has caused. After yawning for the fifth time, he says goodnight and I go inside. Thankfully I'm exhausted from the long day and fall asleep right away. As I drift off, a pair of intense green eyes is the last thing I see.

CHAPTER THREE

Dane

Beep beep beep.

Moaning, I pull my pillow over my head hoping to drown out that irritating noise.

Beep beep beep.

Beep beep beep.

"Ugh . . ." Smacking my alarm silent, I toss my pillow to the side and grudgingly roll out of bed. You would think years of helping out on my parents' ranch would prepare me for the early mornings, but they haven't gotten any easier. Especially now that I'm running it and need to be the first one up. Even in the summer, I'm out of the house before the first light is even a sliver over the hills.

Looking out of my window at the stars twinkling before they are out for the day, my eyes are pulled to Emma's place. The house is dark and silent, a black shadow in the light of the moon. The guy that called her, Alex—my mind spits out his name like it is toxic—that's an unexpected complication, yet she said she had no boyfriend so maybe he's her gay best friend or something. The name rings a bell but I can't think why and I don't want to ask Lia because that will lead to an hour of teasing.

Quickly dressing, I head to the barn to saddle up Charger and go check on the horses. Hopefully Samson hasn't broken them out again.

A soft whinny greets me as I push the door all the way open and turn on the light. Charger pops his head over the gate at the end of the barn, ready to get started.

It doesn't take long to have him geared up and on the trail. The morning air is fresh and I breathe deeply, enjoying the birds rustling as they wake up, a soft light building on the horizon.

The rolling acres of the ranch always gives me a sense of peace as I ride in the morning. We have worked hard as a family to have one of the most prosperous horse ranches in Alberta. Our Quarter Horses are well-bred and highly sought after. Patting Charger with pride, I stop him at the top of the hill, admiring the small valley before us and the faint outline of the Rocky Mountains in the distance.

Kicking Charger into motion, we lope towards one of the wells. It was leaking and we had to shut it down until we could repair the pipe. I finally got word from the plumber that it was replaced late yesterday.

"Shhh." I stop Charger and go to check the clipboard left inside the well-house. Looking over the work order, I make a note that I've turned the well back on. Now that it's fixed and the fence is almost completely replaced we will be able to move the mares and their babies back in. It pisses me off having to replace the fence when we have so many foals, but Mother Nature had other plans. Thankfully none of the babies were hurt when the trees came crashing down during the last thunderstorm.

The rest of my morning rounds go quickly, my thoughts wandering frequently to the beautiful brunette living next door.

Spending the evening with Emma did nothing but increase my desire for her. She has changed since childhood, but only for the better. Time hasn't made her lose her spunk and she still has a passion for the people she cares about and the land that surrounds us. It breaks my heart to see her so sad. I want to cleanse her of the sadness that radiates off her and make her smile all the way to her beautiful green eyes. Lia said she changed a lot after her parents passed away, growing quieter and more cautious although I have yet to see that because she always has a quick remark for me.

Charger and I exit the trails and my eyes are drawn to movement in the pen where her horses are. Her mares are stunning and they are trotting together around the pen. As they turn towards me, I see Emma jogging in between them.

Heart pounding, I watch the woman who has never left my dreams. She waves as she slows to a walk, lifting my hand in acknowledgment I abruptly dismount and turn Charger towards the barn.

I have an idea.

～

Emma

Rubbing my eyes as I stretch, the fact that I slept fully through the night dawns on me. I've woken up at least three times a night since my parents' accident.

The anxiety still holding onto me makes me feel weak and ashamed so I never told anyone about the nightmares, not even Alex. I was horrified when he found out one night. He had slept in my guest room and was woken by my screams and sobs.

He also knows about the car anxiety because he was witness to a full-blown panic attack while driving me in his car one day. After that he worked patiently with me so that I could drive in my truck with minimal anxiety and can sit in the front passenger seat of his car for short periods of time.

Alex tried to convince me to try anti-anxiety medication, but I want to work through it on my own. He worries about me and I appreciate that, but it's not easy to talk about. The sympathetic looks people give you, or when they see you and quickly walk in the other direction because they just don't know what to say. It's humiliating.

Alex is the only one who knows about my anxiety; I have kept it to myself and hope to continue to do so. I don't want people to treat me differently or look at me with even more pity in their eyes; the poor broken girl who fears attachments, vehicles, and has nightmares because she cannot cope with loss. No thank you. I always thought I was stronger, but the past year has worn that strength away.

Glancing at the clock, I'm glad to see I haven't slept in too late. Throwing on some yoga pants and a tank top before walking to the window to look outside, I enjoy the scene before me. It's a beautiful morning and I can tell it's going to be scorching hot by this afternoon.

Turning away, I quickly wash up and brush my teeth before grabbing a banana on my way out the door. Chloe trails closely behind me as we are greeted by Serenity and Belle at the gate. I let myself in and start jogging.

It was shortly after my parents' accident that I got in the

habit of a morning jog with all three of my girls and Chandler. It gave me the opportunity to ensure they hadn't injured themselves overnight, but it also cleared my head of the nightmares.

Despite the lack of nightmares last night, I still love the whoosh of air as you run and the freeing feeling that comes with it. My legs begin to burn as we circle around the paddock for the third time and I feel a smile grow on my face, I haven't felt this at peace in a long time and I know it's being back at the one place I always considered home.

As I round back towards the gate I see Dane sitting on a magnificent horse looking at me. Faltering a step before attempting to casually wave a greeting at him, he waves back before dismounting and heading into their barn. Releasing a breath I didn't know I was holding, I hug Serenity.

"What am I going to do about this crush?" I whisper to her. She nuzzles me comfortingly and I promise her we will go for a ride after breakfast. Moving to stand next to Belle, I give her a long hug and whisper to her before calling Chloe to my side.

Together we head over to see Lia for our breakfast date. I'm hopeful she won't have picked up on my crush. Despite only spending a very limited amount of time with Dane, he has forced his way into my core and is ever present in the back of my mind.

If I think about it though, he has always been there. A lingering memory of how close we once were. The hope I would feel when we would come visit Grandpa instead of him coming to us, only to discover the boys had gone camping or to some training course. The Hyatts were always there in the memories of my happiest moments from childhood. Over time the memories weren't quite so prevalent, and as I grew I found myself focusing on my family and Alex.

I'm not one to form quick attachments, so these abrupt feelings of attraction are overwhelming and I need to figure out what to do about them. Hopefully I wasn't too obvious in watching his movements and analyzing his looks. Lia has a sixth sense about these things, I know it won't be long before she figures it out, but maybe, just maybe, I can contain it before she realizes I'm swooning over her big brother. Not that she would take issue with it; in fact, she would jump on that band-wagon so fast we would probably have some effed up name combination like Danem or EmDane. As children, she used to dream about me marrying one of her brothers so we could be sisters.

I knock on the door and scratch Chloe behind the ear cooing at her while I wait.

"Come in!" I faintly hear Lia holler. Opening the door. I follow my nose to the kitchen. My eyes are automatically drawn to the table which is loaded with food and my jaw drops.

"How many of us are you feeding?" Reaching across the table to grab a strawberry, I peer at her wide-eyed, before popping it in my mouth.

"First of all, never knock when you come over. Ever. You're family." She glares at me and elicits a grin as I chew. "And second of all, have you seen Dane and Ryan pack away the food? I'm used to cooking big." Grabbing another strawberry, I lean over and give her a quick hug. They are so lucky to have each other. As an only child, after I moved away I was so lonely, at least until Alex moved in with us two years later.

"True enough. I'm only used to cooking for myself, or me and Alex. Speaking of my friend Alex, he is moving up here." I wink at Lia suggestively. "I think you two would hit it off . . ."

Lia rolls her eyes at me and grins. "Who has the time?" Smirking at her, I call Chloe from her exploration of the house and get her to lie down beside me.

I start to stuff a piece of bacon into my mouth when I hear

the back door open. Tensing as I turn, I can't help the whoosh of a relieved sigh that sounds from my mouth when I see it's Ryan. Ignoring Lia's inquisitive look, I jump up to give Ryan a hug.

"How's it going?" He grins as I pull away.

"Good, except with all this food you're going to have to roll me out of here." He laughs and starts to load up his plate while eyeing me. "You need to put some weight on, you're too skinny."

Rolling my eyes, I load my plate full of food and munch on some bacon with a pointed look in his direction. He grins with an approving nod.

"Since you're off, maybe we can head into town today. I need to stock the house." Dane walks in as I'm talking, our eyes locking.

"If you can hold off on driving to town until tomorrow, we'll all go," he says as he takes the seat next to me and starts loading up a plate. It might just be my imagination but it seems like he pulled his chair closer to mine.

Softly inhaling a calming breath as Dane's close proximity shoots tingles up my arm, I look at Lia to ground myself and by the eyebrows lifting into her hairline, I don't think I imagined it. She slowly grins as she looks between us.

Oh man, I can see the matchmaking plan building in her brain. Squinting my eyes in a suspicious glare, I shake my head, but she chooses to ignore me.

"Yeah, let's all go together!" she agrees. Nodding slowly, I try to think of how I will convince them to let me drive.

"Will you please pass me the bacon?" Dane's deep voice in my ear causes a shiver to run down my spine. I cover it up by grabbing the bacon and handing him the plate. His fingers linger over mine and my breath catches as heat runs through my body, my heart picking up its pace. He pauses and I wonder if he felt it too. Making sure he has the plate, I quickly pull my hand away and resume eating as nonchalantly as possible, my fingers continuing to shoot tingling sensations up my arm.

"Tomorrow works fine, maybe today you can help me unpack some more?" I ask Lia. She nods and silence falls as we focus on eating. Dane's nearness is making it hard to concentrate so I try to casually shift my chair away from him. Out of the corner of my eye I see his lips twitch as they fight a smile. Damn, caught. This is not helping the torrent of feelings I've discovered since coming back into his life.

"What do you boys have planned for today?" Lia asks breaking into my thoughts.

"I have five horses to trim today then going to Mom and Dad's to do some work around the yard," Ryan says around his mouthful of pancake. I laugh at the look of disgust on Lia's face before she turns to Dane.

Dane grins at her and makes a point of finishing his mouthful before responding. "I was thinking of asking Em here if she wanted to ride around the property with me." He looks at me and winks. "It's been a while and I thought you might like to become reacquainted."

I barely restrain my jaw from dropping. Is he flirting with me? Doubtful, he's just being playful. Realizing everyone is staring at me, I shake off my shock and casually nod. I know if I tried to verbalize my agreement it would come out sounding all breathy and that would be mortifying.

He smiles wide at me and my heart flutters. I smile back at him unable to help myself and finish my breakfast. I need to get a handle on these feelings. I'm not ready to let anyone into my life intimately, I need to focus on finding my new normal first.

"So, Lia, this afternoon why don't you come over then and we can catch up?" I look up at her from my plate, catching her smug smile. She presses her lips together trying to restrain herself and nods. I know I'm going to be interrogated about my ride with Dane when she visits later. Ride . . . Dane . . . okay, seriously, I need to stop!

We wrap up breakfast and I help Lia clean up despite her protests. It's the least I can do when she has fed me twice now.

As I'm finishing with clean up Dane says, "Em, I will meet you outside in twenty minutes, okay?"

"Great!" My voice is pitched a little high, so I clear my throat and tone down my smile. Drying my hands, I give Lia a quick hug and head out the door.

The thought of going riding with Dane makes me nervous, but underlying that, excitement floods my senses. It has been a long time since I have toured their massive ranch and it will feel good to be outside enjoying the grace and beauty of the land and horses.

Just thinking about spending the morning with Dane also has me a little giddy, but I try to tone that down. Simply contemplating pursuing him when he may not be interested makes me anxious, but the thought that the feelings could be reciprocated is worse. If anything were to jeopardize the easy relationship I have with any of the Hyatts, it would be getting involved with Dane.

History does not bode well for people being able to handle my anxiety, panic attacks, and nightmares. Case in point, Johnathan, the ex. He got up the morning after my first nightmare and said he couldn't deal with my grief and anxiety; it was too much for him. Honestly, it was time for things with him to end, but that made me realize I needed to deal with my shit before being in a relationship was an option.

With renewed determination to curb these feelings for Dane, I get ready for our outing. Carefully choosing a pair of comfortable jeans and a light, long sleeved shirt over top of a tank top, I mentally prepare myself to ignore the way he makes me feel and pray that instead we can find the easy friendship we once shared.

Twenty minutes later Dane and I are mounting our horses and he is leading the way onto some new trails they have cut through the forest. He talks about the work they have done around the land, including increasing the training program he and Ryan started. It's fascinating how quickly they have expanded their breeding program to include a starting program for the foals bred here.

We've been riding for a few hours, Dane updating me on the changes to the ranch trails, spending a significant amount of time helping me reacquaint myself with navigating them. When exploring this much land, it's crucial to understand how to find your way back.

It's been relaxing and I enjoy feeling Serenity's ease as she moves beneath me, while watching how expertly Dane leads us through the bush trails filling the property. After Dane finishes explaining the logistics of finding my way about the ranch, a comfortable silence falls between us and I relax significantly into the quiet.

I'm looking around me when I catch Dane's eyes as he looks back at me. Something in his expression shifts the atmosphere and it feels as though every nerve in my body is on high alert. "How does it feel being back here?" Dane breaks the silence causing me to jump. He chuckles as he returns his gaze to the trail ahead.

Serenity snorts at me as I reply, "It feels amazing actually. I said to Ryan last night that it's where I feel connected to them the most. I haven't felt this at peace in a while." Fading off, I hope he doesn't inquire and breathe a sigh of relief as he remains silent for a beat.

"I can't even imagine what you have gone through this

past year, Em. I know we're all happy to have you back." He pauses, turning to grin at me. "I didn't realize just how much I missed you until I was pulling you out of the water trough." I gape at his back as he turns Charger, his horse, to climb a hill at the top of which I can see a clearing.

Taking a deep breath before responding, I say, "I missed you guys too. I kept in contact with Lia, not sure what happened with you and Ryan." Clumping them all together makes saying that I missed him safer because I have missed him.

At one time Dane and Lia were my best friends. We did almost everything together and I remember how disappointed I was when I visited last and Dane wasn't home. Part of me knew that he would have changed since seeing him, but spending time with him now, he is the same Dane, just older, sexier, and more confident.

Pulling out of my reverie, I realize we have made it to the clearing and I gasp at the scene before me. Dane has hopped off Charger and grins at my reaction. I walk Serenity further into the clearing, all the while taking in the quiet creek running through it and breathing the scent of peppermint that is growing all around us. My mind races back to playing tag, wading in the creek, and campouts with Dane and Lia in this very spot. It was also the spot I ran to when I needed to be alone and think.

"I can't believe you remembered how much this spot means to me," I whisper, mostly to myself, but I know he hears me when he smiles at me softly. Walking Serenity over to him, I stop within a few feet to dismount. Before I can swing my leg around Dane walks over and grips my hips, pulling me gently down. Holding my breath, I avoid eye contact as I slide down his body as he lowers me smoothly to the ground.

Tingling spreads through me as my breasts brush his chest.

He has no idea what he does to me and the second he looks into my eyes he will see it written there. Feet planted on the ground, his hands still resting on my hips, I compose myself before looking at him.

"Well, don't I feel like a princess!" I smirk trying to disguise what his proximity is doing to me. He is staring intensely into my eyes and it's all I can do to not lean in and swipe my lips against his. Pulling away I soften my tone. "Thank you so much for bringing me here."

Dane sighs and runs his hand through his hair. "I thought you would appreciate it. I brought us a picnic so we could spend some time here." He gestures to the saddle bag on Charger's back and smiles at me.

"That sounds wonderful." I'm getting a frustrated vibe from him and I don't understand why he would be annoyed, yet I smile and try to be appeasing. "This ride has been amazing and I love the picnic idea. It's like old times. Thank you for thinking of it." He seems to shake whatever is bothering him off and turns to the saddlebag, pulling containers out of it.

Wandering over to the creek, I yank my boots off and dip my toes in while he lays out a blanket and assortment of goodies. The cool water feels divine on my feet and I let my thoughts wander.

This place holds so many memories and it's an overload for the senses. The time we attempted to make a tree house and Ryan broke his arm because the base fell out of the tree, holding Dane and Lia's hands as we waded in the creek, and my favorite memories of our families camping out here.

I'm startled out of memory lane when Dane calls me over to the spread he has set out. Looking down expecting a small assortment of treats and instead seeing enough food to feed several people, I look at him shocked. He laughs that deep, rumbly laugh that sets my core on fire when he sees the expression on my face.

Sitting down, I try to think of anything else but how turned on his laugh makes me, clenching my thighs to alleviate the ache in my body. He is sitting next to me, his arm brushing against mine and I can tell he is waiting for my reaction, so I examine the food more closely and ignore my body. All the food are my favorites. There is apple pie, cherries, punch, strawberries, cookies n' cream chocolate, and that's just the start.

"I can't believe you remembered all my favorites!" Awed at what is before me, his thoughtfulness has rendered me speechless. It's been thirteen years and he still remembers all the necessities for our picnics.

"Well, don't just stare at it! Eat!" he demands.

Shaking myself, I tease him back. "Bossy aren't you?" I smirk at him as I pop a cherry into my mouth.

He grins wickedly at me. "I can be," he says winking suggestively. Choking as I laugh and shake my head. It's so easy to be around Dane, I'm more relaxed than I have been in a long time.

We sit in companionable silence as we munch away and enjoy the sun, scents, and quiet of the clearing. The Chick-a-Dees are chirping away and I can hear a Woodpecker in the distance.

Once I have eaten until I'm stuffed, I lay back with a sigh and start pointing out shapes in the clouds just like we used to. Dane lies next to me, our sides pressed together.

Moving my hands to rest on my belly, I try to think of something to say. This moment feels intimate and it's wreaking havoc on my nerves. A burning sensation alerts me to Dane's eyes on me and I turn my head towards him. His green eyes search mine, for what I don't know.

Unable to handle the lingering eye contact, I'm searching for something to say when a shrill ringing by my side disrupts the peace of the nature surrounding us, scaring the ever-loving crap out of me.

"Holy shit!" Sitting up abruptly, I look down and notice Dane's cell by my foot ringing persistently into the quiet. I silently pass it to him, but not before noticing the name on the screen.

It's Yvette. He looks at the phone and shuts it off. I'm confused by her calling him as I thought he wasn't seeing her anymore and it's a splash of cold water on the warm and fuzzy feelings this picnic was building onto my crush.

"Sorry about that." He smiles apologetically but the moment has passed and I suggest we head back. Avoiding looking at him, I start packing up. When he continues to sit there, I finally meet his steady gaze. Whatever he reads in my eyes answers the question in his and he reluctantly nods.

Later that afternoon Lia and I are organizing my closet when she finally mentions my ride with Dane.

"So—" she starts, "How was your ride with my brother this morning?" She winks suggestively at me and I roll my eyes.

Lia has always been like this, a hopeless romantic, despite the fact that her high school sweetheart ripped out her heart two years ago. Since then Lia hasn't had much dating history because she does not want to open herself up to being hurt again. I sincerely hope that when the right guy comes along, she is able to allow herself some vulnerability and open her heart. However, when it comes to trying to fix others up she will do whatever she can to help them find their happiness. We are both similar in this way.

"It was good, nice to get out for a ride and explore. We stopped for a picnic in our old clearing. It was amazing . . ." Trailing off I think about how surprised I was at the thoughtfulness of the entire outing. Dane didn't need to say he had missed me and thought of me, he showed it through his gesture.

"But . . ." Lia prompts, trying to hide the look of disappointment at my tone.

"We're friends and nothing more. Even if I wanted to explore more it's too much of a risk. Besides, while we were eating Yvette called and I'm not into breaking up relationships or flirting with other women's men."

Lia scowls at the mention of Yvette. "He is not still seeing that woman. She just doesn't know how to take no for an answer. If my opinion is worth anything, if you feel anything more than friendship for Dane, go for it."

Smiling at her regretfully, I distract her with my impressive closet and asking about massage therapy for Belle. At the mention of working with my horses she becomes animated and relief flows throw me that my distraction worked.

CHAPTER FOUR

Dane

Rolling out of bed, I'm still pissed the fuck off at Yvette for calling me yesterday. That woman does not know how to take a hint. We had our three dates, it didn't click and I told her it wouldn't work. Only one woman has made it past the three dates and she totally fucked me over, so now I'm even more selective.

If I'm being honest with myself, I know I've been holding out for Emma and the fact that Yvette put our afternoon to an end enrages me. The look in Emma's eyes, the shields going up that have never been there before, sliced into my heart. She is going to be a tough nut to crack.

Rushing out the door, I hurry through my chores so we will be ready to head into the city. Despite being close to some small towns, we're making the long trek into Edmonton for our monthly restock. It's a full day trip and I'm hoping to make up what I lost yesterday. Pulling out my phone, I decide I need to deal with Yvette. Enough is enough. Typing out a text, I read over it a few times to make sure it's not rude, but direct enough that maybe she will finally back off. Satisfied with the words, I hit send.

> Me: Seriously Yvette, I don't know how many times I need to tell you that I'm not interested. Please stop calling and texting, it's not going to happen. Not now, not ever.

Will she actually stop this time? Who knows, that woman has a few screws loose and it was very apparent by the third date. That rule may seem callous to some, but holy shit has it come in handy. Not that I need it anymore, my heart made its decision a long time ago. I just need to get her to cooperate.

Lia is in the kitchen packing snacks for the drive. Pouring myself a coffee, I sit at the breakfast bar and inhale the heavenly scent wafting from my mug.

"Are you still seeing Yvette?" Lia asks as she lifts the cooler bag onto the counter. Interesting . . . Emma must have mentioned the interruption yesterday.

"Hell to the fucking no. Woman doesn't know when to let go! I texted her this morning, again, to tell her to move on, but who knows. I just pray she doesn't show up here because she tends to get a little handsy."

Making a gagging motion, Lia gives me a "you're an idiot" look. "Maybe you should block her phone number."

"You're right, I didn't even think of it." Pulling my phone out, I scroll to her number and block it before deleting the contact.

Lia mutters about stupid men before slapping the shopping list down on the counter. "Anything I'm missing?" Scanning the list, I add a few things and pass it back to her. She looks over what I added and snaps her head up with a knowing grin.

Rolling my eyes, I stick my mug in the dishwasher and walk out of the kitchen. I love my sister, but I see the wheels turning in her head and that often means meddling. I seriously hope one day the tables are turned on her. Man, will that be fun!

~

Emma

The sun is barely breaking the horizon when I walk over to the Hyatt's. They are already ready to go and as we leave the house I casually suggest we take my truck, however I am unanimously vetoed.

"We have a nice car for commuting; it has a huge trunk and won't eat your gas. We're taking that," Dane says with finality.

It's no use arguing with him so I quickly shout, "Shot gun!" Lia groans and pokes Ryan to get in the back while winking at me. Relieved, I crawl into the front seat and take the deep cleansing breaths I practiced with Alex.

Throughout the drive I do my best to laugh at Lia and Ryan's antics while ignoring the questioning looks Dane is sending my way. I know I'm not acting like myself by not jumping in on the conversation, but the first time driving with someone always requires a lot of focus. One day it won't be necessary but I'm just not there yet.

I hate that I'm so weak to allow my parents' car accident to impact me like this, I wasn't even in the damn car! Alex has told me countless times that I am strong and it is an understandable reaction when they couldn't even save the bodies of my parents from the wreckage. Larger vehicles have come to mean safety and small cars, like this one, bring on an image of my parents' sedan wrapped around a tree, crushed underneath the hood of the semi-truck that t-boned them.

The loss of my parents shocked me to my core and every day I have something I wish I could share with them. The ache in my chest has not lessened and the only way I have been able to get through the past year is with Alex by my side and pretending everything is okay. I know I can't continue this way, but I don't know what else to do.

Feeling my breath hitch at these thoughts, I scrunch my eyes shut and picture galloping through a field with Serenity. Imagining the wind blowing my loose hair out behind me, the feel of Serenity's smooth gallop and the blur of the scenery as we fly across the field helps to calm the anxiety and sorrow building in my mind. This is my happy place and it's where I need to go to clear these thoughts and stop the panic attack in its onset.

Continuing to picture this in my mind, I guide us into the trees. As my imagination fills my mind with pictures, I feel the panic subside and almost forget that I'm in a small car. During these times Alex knows to give me my silence until I'm ready to open my eyes.

But I'm not with Alex.

Dane clears his throat and whispers, "Are you okay, Em? You're looking a little pale."

Nodding and opening my eyes to look at him, "I'm fine, just trying to think of what all I need to get in town." He looks at me skeptically as I barely stop the reflexive cringe that comes when I lie. Attempting a smile to ease his concern, I turn and look out the window. Lying is something I despise and therefore am terrible at, but I don't want them to see inside my messed up brain. Only Alex knows and he has barely scratched the surface.

The rest of the three and a half hour drive northeast to Edmonton passes quickly and I concentrate on participating more actively in the conversation, putting an end to Dane's inquiring looks. As we run our errands, the ease in which we interact makes it feel like no time has passed between us, even though I have only been back in their lives for a couple of days. Lia admits she kept Ryan and Dane in the loop over the years, especially after we both got hooked on social media.

"We all missed you and, until recently, both Ryan and Dane have avoided Facebook; so I would show them pictures and what not," Lia says to me almost guiltily.

"I'm glad you shared, I never post anything I don't want out there anyways." As we pack the rest of the trunk with enough supplies to last us at least a few weeks I feel my relaxed state dissipate. Lia had mentioned to me while we shopped that whoever sat in the front seat always sits in the back on the way home in order to be fair. Ryan and Dane split the responsibility of driving so Dane and I would be in the back for the ride home.

I'm not sure what it is about being in the back seat of a vehicle, but ever since the crash I cannot handle it. Alex and I didn't practice that as it was never necessary since we only ever travel as a pair.

Contemplating whether or not I can pretend to sleep in order to go to my happy place for the whole ride, I reluctantly slide into the car, my throat already feeling constricted.

As we all get buckled in, I'm picturing taking Belle out instead of Serenity. I rarely ride Belle anymore because she has some arthritis in her back legs, but on occasion we will go out and those moments are cherished by us both.

Everything is going well until we start moving. As we leave

the city and speed up to the highway limit, it gets more and more difficult to stay in my happy place. Scrunching my eyes closed even tighter while gripping my hands into the seat, I guide Belle and me through a heavily treed trail. The birds are singing and there is a cool breeze. All around us is the scent of spruce trees, moss and fresh rain.

The car picks up even more speed and visions of my parents' crumpled sedan start flashing through my mind. We sway a bit as a semi-truck passes us and sweat breaks out onto my forehead as the panic starts to rise. I feel closed in, I can't see the road ahead of me and the back of the car seems to shrink as I count my breaths. All attempts at staying in my happy place are forgotten as I try to hold myself together.

I don't want to see the wreckage in my mind anymore. The pain it causes is crippling and I want to be strong. Fear of letting anyone glimpse inside the reality of my grief has me trying to refocus. In my heart I know I can't stop the panic attack, but that doesn't stop me from trying, it can't.

Pressing the palms of my hands against the side of my head, I faintly hear Dane trying to talk to me against the roar in my ears. Ignoring him, I refocus on my imaginary ride with Belle. I imagine us walking into a valley that has a stream flowing through it. We stop for a drink of water and I cool my feet off as I stretch out along the bank. Belle's quiet presence is a comfort to me in the silence of nature as we relax in the sun.

The car shudders as another semi-truck passes us and my attempts at remaining with Belle in my mind fails once again. My breathing becomes erratic as the feeling of not enough air and panic rushes through me. Sweat pours down my face and I can feel the tears start to flow when my mind fills with scenes from the accident a little under a year ago. The pictures in my mind are as vivid and devastating as the day I was called about the accident.

Dane's frantic voice breaks through to me as I hear him calling my name. I also hear Lia and Ryan through the rush in my head asking what the hell is going on. Too far gone to respond, I curl into myself and let the panic attack take hold.

My body is shuddering as I fight for breath when a muttered curse breaks through the panic and pain into my brain. Warmth meets my side as I feel Dane slide over the seat to put his hand gently on my back as though he is afraid to startle me.

The moment my brain registers the contact, the circles that his hand is rubbing over my back soothingly, the shuddering stops and oxygen starts to flow freely in my lungs again. Gasping at the free flow of air, I'm reeling from the abrupt change in my body. His hand stills for a moment at the unexpected shift before continuing its circles.

My mind is in shock. One gentle touch from Dane and the panic is gone. The tears slow and my thoughts clear of the painful scene that was running through them. Without thinking I curl into him exhausted and pass out.

Dane

Emma is out cold, head resting awkwardly on my chest. Gently, I lower her to my thigh and continue to rub circles over her back, ignoring my body as it reacts to her closeness. Her heavenly scent encircles me and I close my eyes to ground myself.

My heart pounds at the emotions flooding through me. I open my eyes and meet Lia's gaze, tears glisten in her eyes as we silently process what happened. Lia reaches over and squeezes my hand before facing the front of the car. This silence won't last long, I can see Ryan is about to blow. He hates feeling out of control and helpless when someone he loves is in pain. I'm shocked he didn't pull over to the side of the road.

Looking down at Emma, her face looks so calm and peaceful considering what just happened, I brush a wisp of hair away from her face.

My mind replays the scene over and over. The shaking, crying, her curled in on herself in actual physical pain. Until I touched her . . . it all stopped when my hand made contact with her. A small smile lifts the corners of my lips. It feels wrong in this moment, but I can't help but feel proud that I was able to quiet her, take away some of her pain even for just a moment.

CHAPTER FIVE

Emma

The car is still moving when I wake up. Realizing I'm curled into Dane, my head resting on his lap with his hand still rubbing circles on my back, I keep my eyes closed. The fact that a simple touch from him immediately stopped my panic attack is still a shock to me and I'll need to dissect that later.

For now, I want to enjoy the close proximity before we go back to friendly non-intimate contact. As I lay there breathing in his woodsy cologne, I finally tune into the conversation of the car and realize that I must not have passed out for long. They are talking about me and what happened. This is what I'm afraid of; I don't want to be the source of people's judgment or, worse, their pity.

"What the hell was that?" Ryan's voice is shaking and it is apparent that what happened shocked him. He's always been the protective bear of the group and I can tell just from his voice that my panic attack has shaken him.

"It seemed like a panic attack to me. There was a girl in school who used to have them and there were a lot of similarities to what was happening to Emma," Lia replies. "I'm guessing it's from being in the car, did you notice how quiet she got each time? I wonder if it's because of the accident." Lia knows me too well. Focusing on keeping my breathing even, I keep listening. It doesn't feel good to eavesdrop on my friends but I need time to prepare myself for the questions I know will come.

"We all saw the photos of the accident, can't say I blame her for not liking cars. I can't believe I forced us to take the car when she suggested her truck." Dane's voice cracks and it takes all I have to not wrap my arms around him. It's not his fault; it's mine for being such a coward.

"How were you to know? I don't think she wanted us to know, otherwise she would have said something." Ryan is always the voice of reason and my heart squeezes for him. I'm not hearing any judgment or pity, just empathy, and relief flows through me. They are so good to me.

This is why I cannot give in to these feelings for Dane. To lose them would break me; the thought of damaging these relationships in any way makes me break out in a cold sweat. The only thing that keeps the panic at bay is Dane's hand rubbing comforting circles over my back. It feels so nice, it's hard not to push into his hand and moan.

"Guys, we should let her talk to us about it in her own time. Dane, I'm looking at you. I know what you want to do and how your personality is, but you can't fix this for her. She'll come to us when she's ready." This is why Lia and I have stayed close. She gets me as well as Alex does without even looking at me. They move on with the conversation and eventually I doze off with the soothing strokes of Dane's hand on my back.

I'm jostled as Dane lifts me out of the car, still half asleep, I wrap my arms around his neck and curl into him, breathing him in. Smiling as I soak up his warmth, I register the sound of him hissing out a rush of air.

My sleep addled brain takes advantage of having Dane's arms around me. I rub my nose up along his neck, keeping my eyes closed as I enjoy the smooth skin up to under his ear. Feeling emboldened in the safety of my feigned sleep, I flick my tongue out to lightly lick the sensitive spot under his earlobe, enjoying the taste of his skin.

A muttered curse makes me smile and I do it again, enjoying the way Dane's breathing has quickened. Part of me feels bad for taking advantage of this moment, but I ignore that thought and glide my nose back down his neck as I nestle back into his shoulder and sigh. Dane presses a kiss to my forehead and I feel myself being lowered gently onto a soft bed. I moan at the loss of his arms but relish in the coziness of the pillow.

The door shuts with a quiet click and I'm alone. Sunbeams caress my skin, their comforting warmth making me drowsy again. I don't want to open my eyes. I want to relish in the moment of selfishness and think about the way it felt to be in Dane's arms. I want to allow myself this moment before I need to face my reality. The reality that I need to work harder on my issues. They're not going away on their own, and being here isn't going to make them disappear, as much as I wish that was the case.

Allowing the warmth of the sun and the comfort of the bed to draw me into sleep, I wrap my arms around the pillow, faintly wondering at the delicious scent of Dane lingering in my room.

Slowly shifting into consciousness, I stretch out on my bed with a content sigh. As my awareness drifts out of me, I realize something feels off. Cautiously opening my eyes, I look curiously around me at the vaguely familiar surroundings that are not my bedroom.

The room is a mixture of bold greens and blues; masculine, simple, and clean. It dawns on me that I'm in Dane's room as I recognize the gabled window looking across to my house. It's been years since I was in Dane's room. When he turned eight he decided girls weren't allowed in there and I haven't been in here since.

Rolling out of his massive king-sized bed I look about his space, cautiously exploring without touching anything. There is not much to see except for some photos on his wall and dresser. The first photo is one of his parents. I gaze at it for a while as I have not seen them since I was sixteen. They look the same as they did when I was last here and it makes me happy to see them so well. When Lia came over to help me unpack yesterday she had informed me that they were away until the fall, travelling the country and enjoying their retirement.

Covering his dresser are more photos of the family, they must have just recently had these done as they all look the same. At the end of the dresser I almost pass by one lone photo, but the sun catching on a silver frame catches my eye and I stop abruptly.

It's me.

And not a photo from when we were kids, those are all on the walls. This is a photo of me from shortly before my parents died. I had hired a photographer to update my author photo and she had taken a great candid of me laughing at something Alex said. He must have gotten this off my Facebook page.

Unsure what to do with this information, I move to examine the photos on the wall. Many of the pictures are from when we were kids, and I laugh at the memories they hold. Familiar photos that also hang in the halls of my house.

Part of me is surprised at how sentimental Dane is. He likes order and control, he was continuously the leader when we were kids. Lia and I always content to follow along with his idiotic and brilliant ideas. To see that his softer side has remained into adulthood warms my heart. The more I get to know Dane again the more my crush strengthens, but so does my resolve to not risk losing the Hyatts. The history we share and sense of family I have with them is more important than the feelings seeing him has stirred up. I would rather bury my attraction than take the risk of acting on my feelings for Dane. And I've become very good at burying how I feel.

Steeling myself against the desire that has not diminished since seeing him, I prepare myself to go downstairs. Pretending I was asleep earlier will be challenging but I need to do it. I better practice my poker face.

Quietly opening the door, I listen for the sound of voices. Silence greets me and I make my way downstairs. Looking at the clock on the wall I deduce that Lia will be in the kitchen preparing dinner so I head that way. Pausing at the door, I listen for Dane's voice. I hate feeling like I need to avoid him, but I still need time to recuperate. Opening the door when I don't hear anything, I walk in.

"Hey, sleepy head! I was wondering if I was going to need to come wake you up. Do you want to stay for dinner?" Lia smiles at me gently, bringing back what happened in the car.

"I don't think so. I'm pretty tired and think I just want to curl up with Chloe. Thank you though." I'm hoping that didn't come across as rude, my brain is still muddled from my panic attack and nap. The thought of cooking for myself is a little daunting in this frame of mind but it's for the best. I think that an evening on my own will give me the time I need to prepare for seeing Dane. Lia is understanding and doesn't push me to stay. God, I love her!

On my way back to the house I check on Belle and Serenity, tossing them some hay. Chloe is sleeping on the porch so I call her in and feed her too. We eat together and then I curl up on the couch with one of the novels I had picked up prior to coming here, Chloe jumps onto the couch and lays at my feet. I settle in for an evening on the couch getting lost in a fictional world. I don't plan on moving from this spot for the rest of the night.

∼

Dane

Adjusting in the saddle, Charger and I continue to herd the mares and foals back to their pen. I watch the foals carefully, and immense pride fills me at how well they're doing. My balls have finally recovered from Emma teasing me in her sleep and trotting isn't quite so painful. Now that I'm not in excruciating pain, I chuckle. I'm still in shock over what happened and thankful I didn't drop her.

The last mare and foal enter the pen so I close the gate behind the horses, dismount and climb up the fence to sit and watch as the horses explore the pen. My mind fills with visions of green eyes and soft lips. Her lips were so soft.

Since we got back from town this afternoon, all I have been thinking about is how to get her to acknowledge her attraction. It's time to make my move and hope that I was the man she was dreaming about.

Jumping down the fence, I grab Charger and we head back home. The sun is setting and I'm hoping Emma is still in my bed.

Charger takes off at a canter, he is eager to eat and relax. He works hard but is rewarded for his hard work too.

As the barn comes in sight, he picks up the pace and I let him go enjoying the exhilarating rush at his burst of speed. He slides to a stop outside the barn and I jump down and quickly pull his saddle off. Trailing behind me into the barn, he walks with me as I put the tack away and grab some brushes.

This is my favorite part of the day, the quiet of the barn mixed with silently brushing my horse after a hard day's work. It truly makes me appreciate what we have. Charger sighs softly as I finish up and lead him to his pen at the back of the barn. Hay is waiting for him and he eagerly goes to eat.

Turning on my heel, I look up at my bedroom window and walk quickly to the house and up the stairs, leaving my boots in the middle of the entryway.

My eyes automatically look to the bed and disappointment floods me when I see it's empty and made.

"Damn." Her soft scent fills my room and I stride to my bathroom so I can quickly wash the day away before I get completely immersed in her.

"What time did Emma leave?" I ask walking into the kitchen for dinner, my stomach gurgles as I inhale the delicious smell of the lasagna that Lia has prepared.

"I would guess about thirty minutes before you walked in the door." Pulling on some oven mitts she reaches in and pulls out cheesy garlic bread that makes my mouth water.

"Why didn't she stay for dinner?" Ryan asks as he starts

mounding food onto his plate. Plopping myself into my chair, I eagerly await Lia's response as I fill my bowl with Caesar salad.

"She didn't say." Damn. Lia wouldn't tell us anyways, she is a fiercely loyal friend and sister. I always loved that about her, until now. Emma fills my thoughts and I zone out as I debate with myself how I can make things better for her. I want to fix her hurts. I want to make her world better.

"Dane!" Ryan's voice pulls me out of my thoughts and I look up to see him smirking at me.

"What?"

"I asked if you got the horses moved okay." He and Lia are both barely restraining their laughter.

"Everything went smoothly." Digging into my food, I pointedly ignore them as they tease me.

"I think the days of his three date rule are over," Ryan says before taking a bite of garlic bread.

"They were over as soon as he heard she was moving back," Lia adds. Lifting my head, I scowl at them. It's not that I care if they know how I feel about Emma or that they are teasing me. I'm frustrated with myself, because I really don't know how to proceed. My gut tells me to proceed with caution but I've never been that type. I charge in at full speed and command things to go my way. That won't work with Emma.

"Dude. You're in la-la land again. What the hell?" Ryan waves his hand in front of my face and I swat his hand away.

"I see what you're thinking, Dane, and it's not going to work. But I think you know that." I look at Lia and cross my arms. The glare is automatic when someone tells me something I don't want to hear.

"I don't know what you're talking about."

"Uh huh. Just listen then. You need to ease in, show your interest and let her process it." Narrowing my eyes at her as I ponder her words, I give Ryan the finger when he opens his mouth with some smartass comment. "You need to be patient. That doesn't mean you can't show your interest, but don't go charging in there expecting to sweep her off her feet."

Lia's words sink in and I nod as we all go back to our food.

I can be patient . . . For a little while.

CHAPTER SIX

Emma

After the incident in Dane's arms, I have tried to maintain some emotional distance. It's not easy; now that I know what it feels like to be in his arms, my body craves more. True to their word, no one has asked me about my panic attack, respecting my need to discuss it in my own time—or not at all.

The next few weeks I set about establishing a normal routine, needing to settle into a familiar groove. Every evening I spend a couple of hours talking to Alex on the phone. He is doing his best to get up here quickly, but he figures it will be at least another week. The thought of seeing him makes me so happy; Alex is this pure and genuine soul. There is no one I have met that can bring me out of my darkest moments like he can, at least until Dane.

Lia has made family breakfast mandatory with the threat of hogtying anyone who doesn't show up and she would too. Dane insists on sitting next to me every morning and has invited me to go on several rides with him. He continues to flirt with me and has progressed from just verbally flirting to tucking my hair behind my ear or resting his hand on the small of my back as I leave a room.

It's been challenging not to give into the desire swirling through my veins, but I have successfully maintained my friend-zone distance. Something tells me women don't refuse Dane often, if at all, and that by not falling at his feet I have become a challenge. If he continues pursuing me I don't know if my resolve will last, especially with the soft touches, smoldering looks, and the genuine interest he has in what I'm saying. I don't think any man has ever been able to make me weak in the knees, intensely turned on, and valued all in one shot.

Thinking back to four days ago, we went back to the clearing as a group for a picnic, when Dane suggested we play a game of touch football. Growing up with Ryan and Dane has made both Lia and I quite good at football but the guys still have speed and power on us. We split in half and Ryan chose me for his team. I had grown to recognize Dane's expressions over the past few weeks and his face had smugness written all over it.

We started the game and were pumped up. Ryan grinned at me as we got in position, him crouched over the ball. He hiked it to me, taking off at a quick run, catching the ball as I threw a perfect spiral. Dane winked at me before taking off after Ryan.

"It's good to see you haven't lost your touch after all these years." Dane nudged me as they came jogging back, a sexy smirk on his face.

"You wish. We all know you've been jealous of my spiral ever since Dad taught me how to throw." I grinned back at him as Ryan tossed me the ball, before returning to my side of the field and huddling up with Ryan.

The day was scorching, so I rolled my tank top up my midriff and tied it in the back. When I stretched my arms over my head, I couldn't help but glance at Dane. His eyes had been glued to my stomach, so at the start of the next play, I had done it again. Ryan laughed as he ran right past Dane, Lia yelling at him to focus.

The first half of the game passed quickly with more teasing and flirting. By the time we decided to quit for lunch, Lia and Dane were down a couple points.

Ryan and I sat on the blanket, spreading out the food. I could see Lia and Dane conspiring as they made their way towards us. Lia had such a smirk, Dane's expression exasperated and yet he continued to gesture and talk to her about whatever scheme she was cooking.

Dane sat close to me on the picnic blanket, his arm brushing mine as the four of us chatted and ate. Electricity shot up my arm every time our skin touched. At one point, a strand of hair fell out of my bun and he brushed it behind my ear, his fingers trailing slowly across my cheek as he pushed the strands out of my face.

He was leaning into me, our eyes locked. The air was heavy and I almost forgot that Lia and Ryan were with us until Ryan laughed at something Lia said. I jerked, and Dane stroked his hand down my arm before he picked up his beer and focused on the conversation Lia and Ryan were holding.

As soon as our picnic was done, the tone of the game changed. Lia was no longer covering me, Dane taking her place. He took every opportunity to get close to me, his large body wrapped around me as he blocked throw after throw.

Ryan tossed me the ball and I was running as fast as I could to score a touchdown when Dane overtook me and tackled me to the ground. He curled his body underneath mine to cushion the fall before rolling me onto my back. My blood coursed through my body like a raging wildfire. I felt hot and flustered as we stared into each other's eyes. It took everything in me not to press into him, to resist lifting my head and kissing him. I knew he had the same thought because his head lowered towards mine. His lips were a breath away when Ryan called to us. Dane froze, his expression disappointed.

"I can't let you score that touchdown," he whispered, "I never give up and I never lose." It felt like there was a double meaning to his words and it ruined the moment for me a little because it made me feel like a conquest.

If Ryan wouldn't have interrupted and if Dane wouldn't have opened his mouth about not losing, I probably would have kissed him. I could feel myself losing to my attraction. Part of me was glad he had given me that reality check but the other part, the little voice in the back of my mind taunting me, told me I had ruined a good opportunity to get him out of my system.

That scene plays over in my head as I get ready to go for breakfast; it has been tormenting me every day. Dane's flirting is wearing me down and I'm not sure how much longer I can hold out.

Reflecting on the conversation Alex and I had the night before, I ponder what he had said. He suggested I start flirting back. He figures it would be a good way to see if it was the chase that was appealing to Dane as he would likely stop if that was the case. That thought scares me too, the temptation is hard to deal with, but to know for sure that I'm a conquest would be painful. I can't believe how many times a day I change my mind on how to deal with Dane and the obvious attraction growing between us.

The more I think about the idea though; I waver on the possibility of changing my tactics. Currently I'm not getting anywhere except stuck inside my head fighting a losing battle, but I'm still on the fence about whether it's a good idea.

My head is muddled with these thoughts as I feed my horses and ensure nothing happened to them overnight. Checking on the girls takes longer than usual because, if I'm being honest with myself, I'm in the avoidance stage of any decision I need to make. As I ponder calling Alex to talk with him I glance over and see Lia stalking purposefully towards me.

"Ahem, breakfast is at eight thirty sharp! It's now eight thirty-five." Her tone of voice is stern, but I see the laughter in her eyes as she scolds me. Unable to prevent the grin that follows those words, we both start laughing.

"I know, I know. I was on my way." Lia looks at me and I can see she is deciding whether or not to say something. "Go on, say what you want to say."

"You have been through so much and I know how scared you are of experiencing more loss. But I see the way you and Dane look at each other, and the way he interacts with you. Why don't you give it a shot? You could be happy. You know, rather than doing this avoidance thing you have going on."

She looks at me expectantly. Opening my mouth, no words come out so I shut it again.

"I know you're worried about it being obvious to Dane but it's not, if that makes any difference." She grins at me.

Breathing a sigh of relief, I meet her eyes. "I just don't know if I can . . ." I whisper. Gazing back at me steadily she nods reluctantly and drops the subject.

In that moment I decide to sit down with her and open up about my fears. She has stood by my side throughout the years and the distance, understanding me every step of the way, and she deserves to know. Plus we haven't had a chance to have any real girl time since I came. There have been several horse emergencies with her clients and after two solid weeks of organizing, cleaning, ordering, and unpacking, my house is finally all settled in.

"Come over this afternoon for some gab time. We haven't had a chance yet and I really want to spend quality time with you." The smile that spreads across Lia's face is contagious. She hugs me and we walk, arms wrapped around each other into the kitchen where Ryan is waiting with a scowl on his face. Lia and I look from Ryan to each other and burst out laughing. His expression says it all: don't keep a man from his food.

We have just started eating when Dane bursts in through the door. Snickering at the look Lia sends him for being late I turn around and say, "There's nothing left for you. I'm eating it all!" I may not be fully decided on how to proceed with my feelings, but I can't help myself from teasing him a little bit.

Grinning while I grab his plate and go to tuck it under the table, I stare him down. He arches a brow at me before lunging towards me. Squeaking, I duck under the table to hand Lia the plate before he has grabbed my ankles and pulled me out. Everyone is laughing until tears are running. I'm smirking at him until I catch the look in his eyes.

"Don't you dare . . ." I start before he begins to tickle me. Laying screaming on the floor in fits of uncontrollable laughter I beg him to stop. This play is different from when he flirts with me. This is what I'm used to with Dane, the way things always were and I love that despite the undeniable attraction I have for him we still have this. He finally stops and I curl up on the floor catching my breath. Crawling to my knees, I allow him to help me up, and smile at the shine of laughter in his eyes. As we sit back down at the table, I glance at Lia as she hands Dane a plate heaping with food. She winks at me and I shake my head.

Over breakfast Lia and I excitedly talk about our girl's afternoon until the guys heads are spinning with chats about mud masks, pedicures, and sexy romance novels.

"When are you starting the final novel?" she asks impatiently.

"I was going to start it soon, but maybe I should hold out

just to tease you a little more." I grin at the scowl that crosses her face. "Or I could start it next week . . ." She grins and does a fist pump in the air.

She talks excitedly about her favorite parts from book one until we're the only two left in the kitchen. Looking at the clock, I start at how much time has passed. "Holy shit! Time flies when you're having fun. I'm going to go work with Serenity for a bit, I will see you at one."

A couple of hours later Serenity and I are making our way out of the trails that wind through my acreage. It was the first time I have explored the ten acres since I was a child and it felt surreal to be riding through there again. I love the peace and quiet of the forest and the openness of my little field.

As I rode and thought about my brief time back home, I realized that my nightmares have reduced to less than three times a week, whereas previously they had been multiple in a night. And the last time we went into town I did not have a panic attack, although that has more to do with Dane holding my hand and sitting next to me the whole time than me actually overcoming my anxiety. I had been able to laugh and joke with everyone, never once needing to retreat into my safe place. Being home is slowly healing me, and I suspect that Dane has a lot to do with it.

I finish my ride in no less of a conundrum of how to approach my attraction to him, his pursuing of me, and the obvious challenge that I am providing for him. The heat that runs through my veins at a simple thought of him hints at more than lust or simple attraction, but I'm good at denying the obvious. I need to talk to Alex again. I miss seeing him every day.

I'm looking forward to spending an entire afternoon vegging out with Lia this afternoon. I know if I talk to her she will give me a different perspective than Alex would. I want to trust her when she says that he looks at me differently, but I also know that her hopes of us getting together may overshadow the truth of what she is seeing. Despite Lia's painful relationship history, she only wants a true love story for those she cares about.

As Serenity and I walk to the paddock I glance over at the house and almost fall out of my saddle. Dane is bathing Charger—shirtless. The muscles of his back ripple as he soaps Charger up and rinses him off. His skin is golden from working outside and the lack of a farmer's tan tells me he often works shirtless.

As I'm staring, he turns around while he works through the tail. Seeing me sitting on Serenity staring at him, he faces me fully and waves with a shout of acknowledgment and knowing smirk. I wave back as I drink in the sight of his well-defined abs from the safety of the distance between us. The man is built, he is book cover worthy and I can't help but envision him on one of my covers.

Realizing I'm still staring, I hop off Serenity and quickly take off her saddle and bridle. Grabbing the brush from the bin by the gate I rub her down while sneaking glances at Dane who has gone back to bathing his horse. How am I supposed to stay away from him? He's funny, extremely attractive, kind, willing to take control, and the way he makes my heart flutter is just unnerving. He is the full package of compassionate and kind, but with the alpha in him that makes my knees weak.

Leading Serenity into the paddock, I glance over to see Lia heading over. I didn't realize how much time had passed so I quickly brush Belle down to give her some attention too and meet Lia by the gate.

"I brought all the staples. Cookies n' cream chocolate, Laffy Taffy, Skittles, and, just for fun, Pop Rocks." She holds up a huge sack of junk food.

"You brought Pop Rocks? Yes!" Those were our choice treats for sleepovers when we were growing up and I cannot wait to relive those memories. We head into the house with Chloe on our heels, reminiscing about previous girl's nights.

An hour later we are surrounded by candy and watching *Dirty Dancing.* We both love the movie and randomly quote our favorite parts. As we're watching I'm trying to decide on how to broach the subject of my anxiety around losing people, and open up about my struggles over the last year. This is a big step for me and I can't help but be a little nervous.

I decide to take the plunge and angle my body towards her. Feeling the shift in my attitude, she pauses the movie and faces me, her posture open.

I take a deep breath.

"Lia, when I showed up at the scene of the accident unaware that my parents were dead, my entire world shattered. You saw the photos from the news article, the car was a pancake. I don't even think they attempted to extricate them from the vehicle. There was no point. Between being flattened by the semi-truck and being squished by the tree, the car was less than half the size it should've been." My eyes blur as I think about that scene. "Not only did I lose my parents, but I don't feel like I've gotten any closure. There was nothing to bury, they are headstones on grass. I know it seems like a morbid thought, but not having that place where I can visit them has added to the massive hole in my chest.

I don't even remember Alex showing up and taking me away from the scene. It's still burned into my memory and, until recently, every time I go to sleep I see it over and over. Sometimes I'm watching the scene of the accident with all the emergency teams. Other times, I'm in the car with them but unable to tell them I love them. At first, I couldn't even go in a car without having a panic attack. What you saw, that day, that was an improvement."

Lia and I stare at each other, tears streaming down our cheeks.

"Then, to top it off, Johnathan decided he couldn't deal with the mess I was, so he broke up with me. Two weeks later, I ran into him with his new girlfriend, a coworker he had been sleeping with on the side."

The only bright spot in my life had been Alex. I recall how he worked with me on my car anxiety so I could sit in the front seat of smaller vehicles. How he dropped everything to stay with me so that when I had nightmares he could come in and comfort me. How his girlfriend left him out of jealousy because she couldn't understand our sibling bond and he never blinked an eye because if she didn't understand then she wasn't the one. He had helped me stabilize myself to the point where I was able to function day to day.

"Alex pulled me through the whole ordeal. He was selfless and steady. He got me to a place where I could get through the day, and then, within the same month, Grandpa passed away. Suddenly, I was completely alone. No family, and a gaping wound that hadn't even had time to heal even just a little. I have this huge chunk missing from my heart and the thought of losing anyone else from my life is more than I can bear."

Lia sobs, reaching a hand out the hold mine as I see the same raw pain I'm feeling on her face. Talking about this, it's like wrenching my pain from deep inside and laying it on the floor for everyone to see. I can't hide from it anymore. It feels good to talk about it, I know I need to more often, but it is still painful.

"Making the decision to move up here was the first time I had felt peace. It gave me something to focus on other than the grief and anxiety, a sense of purpose. I'm lucky that my job allows me the flexibility to take a break and coming up here has been healing. I don't have the nightmares every night anymore, I can ride in the car, and when I think about my parents the pain is lessened because I have the sense of family and connection that I needed. I'm starting to be able to think of them with the happiness of memories, instead of searing pain.

"But, Lia, you guys and Alex are all that I have left in terms of family. The thought of doing anything to lose that tears me apart and I don't know that I could recover from it. It's too much."

She takes a deep breath as she wipes her eyes. "I cannot imagine how horrifying that was for you. And I wish I had been able to do something to help." She holds up a hand as I start to protest, "No, Em, the phone calls weren't enough. But I've seen how Dane calmed you in the vehicle, and how you look at each other. You can't deny the attraction, plus the impact he has had on your healing."

"You're right; he has helped, a lot. I'm not denying it. But what if I'm just someone who hasn't given in to his charm? You know me too well to pretend I don't have feelings for him, but I'm scared to act on them. I can't lose you guys too!"

"Emma, Dane doesn't play those kinds of games. If you were just a conquest, he would move on. There are plenty of women who would be willing to have a one-night stand with him. Now, onto the more important point. There is nothing, NOTHING that could ever happen to cause you to lose us."

I give her a hard hug and whisper, "I will think about what you're saying. I will. Thank you, I love you."

"I love you too." The thing I love about Lia is that she knows when to stop. She starts the movie up again and we go back to our girl time.

A few hours later we have eaten more than our fill of junk food, finished watching *Dirty Dancing* and *Pitch Perfect*. When I had found out that Lia hadn't seen *Pitch Perfect*, I made it mandatory for her to stay and watch it.

We both stretch and groan at our full bellies. The afternoon has been wonderful. It feels like a weight has been lifted off my shoulders by opening up to Lia. The afternoon was what I needed. I'm so much more relaxed about the Dane situation, despite still not having come to a decision, things feel a little clearer. It was also nice pampering myself with a pedicure and facial.

Lia stands and stretches. "I better get going, I need to cook supper for when the guys get home." We walk to the door and I give her a hug.

"Thank you for understanding. I'm glad I opened up; Alex is always telling me I need to talk about it more. I hate it when he's right." She squeezes me again before heading home.

∼

Dane

I'm tired of waiting.

CHAPTER SEVEN

Emma

Setting the dishwasher, I top up my wine and call Alex for our nightly chat. I'm spent from my afternoon with Lia, but I also feel a little lighter. The weight I'm bearing is becoming a little more tolerable every day.

"Hey, Emma. How's your night going?" It sounds like he's driving, the recognizable road noise in the background.

"Good—are you driving?" Glancing at the clock on my wall, my brown furrows when I see how late it is.

"Umm, yeah. I just had to run out and grab some more packing tape." His voice shifts, becoming weird and stilted. The way it does when he's lying.

"At eleven o'clock at night?" My voice betrays my skepticism. It's rare that Alex lies to me, and it's usually when he doesn't want to burden me with something that happened with his piece of shit mother.

"Yeah. So, you've been home for quite some time now, have

you started your book yet?" The abrupt change of subject doesn't alleviate my suspicion. When I don't answer right away, Alex scolds, "Emma, you need to write. Stop procrastinating and get back to work. You know you need to."

"Okay, okay. I know, you're right. It will be nice when you're here, we can lounge around my living room getting our work done together."

"Soon. I promise. In the meantime, you need to motivate yourself." His voice shifts, amusement filling his voice.

"Fine. I will boot up my laptop now. I love you. I can't wait to see you."

As soon as we hang up, I run upstairs to change into my typical writing attire. My well-loved sweats and retro *Mario* t-shirt are ratty and old, but they are incredibly comfortable. Grabbing my laptop from my office desk, the same place it has sat untouched since the day I moved in, I settle onto the couch and boot it up.

It's time to stop putting off starting my new book, I know Alex is right. Opening a blank document, I stare at the empty page, the blinking cursor mesmerizing as I try to find my opening sentence.

Blink. Blink. Blink. Blink.

I finish my wine, so I top it up again and continue to stare. My notes are open in a separate doc, so I flip there and read through what I had plotted.

Blink. Blink. Blink.

Sighing, I throw my head back and groan. The story isn't flowing like it usually does in the beginning; instead my mind is being pulled into a million new directions. I know I need to get started on the final book of my current series but those characters are just not speaking to me.

Clearing my head, I decide to just type. Type whatever comes out. My fingers start to fly over the keyboard as something entirely different begins to take shape now that I'm allowing myself to write what wants to be written.

A couple of hours pass and the story that has begun to unfold is familiar to me, it's reminiscent of the emotions swirling through me about Dane. Stretching my arms above my head as I read over the last paragraph, I abruptly shut my laptop in frustration.

The story is something I can work with, but I'm feeling flustered by the constant presence Dane has in my mind. His relentless lingering in my thoughts is wearing on me. I'm sitting staring at my laptop, pondering my conversations with Lia and Alex, when a knock sounds at my door. Chloe looks up from my feet and growls a bit but I hush her. Way out here, I can almost guarantee it's one of the Hyatts. Getting up, I set my laptop aside and hurry to get the door, glancing at the clock on my way, midnight. Odd, I hope everything is okay.

Swinging the door open, I gape as I take in Dane standing on my stoop. Unable to resist checking him out, my eyes run over his body. He is wearing sweat pants that accentuate his muscular thighs and well-defined bulge. My body heats up at the sight, his pants leaving little to the imagination, and I quickly move up examining his black t-shirt to his grinning face.

He hands me a carton of ice cream, smirking as I feel the tell-tale burn of embarrassment.

"Aren't you going to invite me in?" He chuckles as I stand frozen in the doorway.

"Of course, come on in." Stepping back from the doorway, I wait while he tucks his boots into the boot rack, and then we walk to the kitchen in silence. My back burns with his gaze.

Grabbing a couple of spoons, I take a few deep breaths before turning in time to see him sit on my couch and grin cheekily at me.

"Nice look, very . . . umm . . . cozy."

Part of my brain is stuck on how good he looks sitting on my couch while the other cringes at how unsexy I look. He continues to smirk at me as his eyes rake over my t-shirt and sweats, the smirk transforms into a full-blown smile as though he can't contain himself.

I narrow my eyes as we watch each other, his gaze full of challenge.

Having him here, in my home, brings up the battle that I've been fighting internally. Should I just sit down and eat ice cream with him, hold everything in, or should I act on my feelings and see where it leads. Anxiety is always at the forefront of my inner struggle, but Lia's words flash through my mind. *I won't lose them, no matter what.*

We both know this is a turning point in our relationship as I waver between my two options. Dane is leaving the choice up to me, and as the grin falters a little the longer I stand here staring at him, disappointment filling his eyes, I can tell he's already decided which choice is going to win.

It's that look of disappointment that makes my decision. I've always hated being predictable, and the huge part of me that wants to see what being with him is like is strong.

A smile spreads across my face as I prowl over to where he is sitting. His eyes widen fractionally and I can tell he can't quite figure out what I'm planning. Stopping in front of him, I drop the ice cream on my coffee table, gather my courage, and, to his shock, straddle him. It's barely discernable, but I see him swallow hard as I sit down right on . . .

Oh my . . .

His reaction to my boldness is apparent and I work hard to keep my features neutral. The feeling of his length hardening beneath me is arousing and resisting reacting to his unex-pected arousal combined with the immediate response of my body is one of the most difficult things I have ever done. Shifting, I sink onto him and shift my hips a little.

"Are you making fun of me?" I whisper looking into his eyes. I can see the heat building there and my heart stutters. Needing to maintain control, I lean forward to press my lips to his ear, grinning as he sucks in a sharp breath.

"I'm not going to give you the satisfaction of riling me up. Two can play this game, and trust me when I say that I can play it better." Dragging myself away from him with attempted nonchalance I grab the spoons and hand him the carton of ice cream. Planting myself next to him on the couch, I wait for him to open the ice cream, but he's staring at me, frozen from shock as his jaw drops a little. He shakes his head a little before tossing the lid to the side and scooping a some of the icy treat into his mouth, a look of determination filling his face as he smiles at me.

When I reach forward to help myself, he snags the spoon from my hand and tosses it to the table. Before the protest has fully left me, his spoon is in front of my lips.

Locking eyes with him, I lean forward and wrap my lips around it pulling back slowly. It's cookies and cream, my favorite.

Closing my eyes, I savor the flavor while attempting to slow the beating of my heart. A gasp slips out as my eyes snap open when I feel Dane's hand on the back of my neck.

His eyes meet mine, searching for something before his lips come crashing onto mine, his hand tightening on the back of my neck when I slide my hands up his hard chest and around his neck.

To say that Dane is an excellent kisser is an understatement, no kiss I have ever experienced comes close to this level. I can feel it all the way to my toes. Everything I have been withholding and denying myself is being released into the pressure of my lips on his.

Our tongues meld together as he deepens the kiss and his free hand pulls me closer as the hand in my hair tugs a little. Moaning, I lean into him trying to get closer.

As he deepens the kiss even more, lips pressing into mine with unrelenting passion, he slides his hands to my ass and lifts me onto his lap. I press into him, wrapping my legs around his waist when he stands from the couch.

He pushes me up against the kitchen wall, his hands kneading my ass as we devour each other. The back of my head hits the wall when he moves his lips to my neck and grinds his hips into me. The feel of his arousal has me soaking wet and my hips moving in response to his, seeking that delicious friction. His mouth moves hungrily over the tender skin of my neck before he nips my ear.

The tension between us builds and I'm almost there when he's suddenly, gently, setting me on the floor with a feather of a kiss on the lips. A growl of displeasure slips out of me and he chuckles. My eyes close as the sound causes my body to tremble with desire.

"This isn't a game to me, Emma. Although, if it were, I think we know who won. That's just something to think about, I'll see you tomorrow." He brushes his lips against mine again and walks away from me.

Keeping my eyes closed, I slump against the wall, only opening them when I hear the door close. Oh my. Sliding down the wall my fingers move to my swollen lips in a daze. My body is throbbing and there is an unsatisfied ache in my core. If Dane can do that with a simple kiss the thought of taking it further makes me tremble in anticipation.

His words resonate within me. A smile grows on my face, maybe we could do this. Is there a possibility that I can have it all with Dane? I finally acknowledge that my feelings for him run deeper than lust, I'm not ready to say I'm in love with him, because let's be real how can it happen that quickly, but if all goes well I could let myself love him as more than a friend. There is no denying that we have the physical attraction to move this past friendship, I've never felt this high after being with someone, never been left craving more so much, that I have to resist the urge to chase after him.

I've been sitting against the wall, frozen in a swarm of thoughts and arousal when a knock at the door startles me out of my internal musings. Jumping up hoping Dane came back to finish what he started, I race to the door and fling it open with a big grin.

My head processes two things at once. It's not Dane, but it is someone I've been needing back in my life.

"Alex!" Hurling myself out the door and into his arms, I breathe in his familiar and comforting scent. He has worn this soft, masculine cologne for as long as I can remember and it reminds me of home.

Alex hugs me hard and tears start to flow down my cheeks. "It's really home now." Stepping back, I take him in. It's been less than a month since I've seen him, but I've missed him tremendously.

His bright hazel eyes shine at me as I examine him closely. He has dark circles under his eyes and I tsk him for pushing himself so hard. His short hair is messy but that is the norm for him, as is the five o'clock shadow that graces his jaw. He is wearing his usual tattered jeans and a t-shirt that shows off the hard work he puts into his body.

Alex works out tirelessly. It's one of the ways he started escaping his mother and he kept it up even after moving in with us. Throwing myself back into his arms for another hug, he laughs as I squeeze him as hard as I can.

"I wanted to surprise you. I was hoping to be here a couple of hours ago but there was a major crash just outside of Jasper. I've already put Chandler in with the girls and tossed them some hay." I pull him inside and shut the door before hugging him for a third time.

This is the longest Alex and I have been apart since he moved in with us. Recalling when he started showing up at our house with burn marks on his arms from his mom's cigarettes makes me squeeze him harder. This man has been through so much in his life and yet he is one of the kindest, most positive and genuine people you will ever meet.

"Are you hungry? I think I have some leftover chicken lasagna in the fridge." Knowing he can't refuse my chicken lasagna I chuckle as he pretends to drool. Before I know it, he has scooped me over his shoulder and is running frantically through the house yelling "Chicken lasagna!" making me laugh one of those full belly laughs. He sets me down once we are in the kitchen and starts scrounging around.

Plopping myself onto a stool, I lean my head onto my hand and watch him. The stress of the long day shows in his hazel eyes but he is smiling and I can tell he feels the shift in me by the light in his eyes as he glances at me while he cuts a large piece of lasagna from the pan. His broad shoulders begin to relax as he sets the microwave and he turns to study the house before returning his focus back to me.

"You look good. This place has done wonders for you." He states it as a fact and I know he doesn't expect a response.

When I left to come up here I had big purple shadows under my eyes and they had lost some of their shine. Even I could see the change the past weeks have brought about in me. As we sit in companionable silence ideas start flowing through me and I quickly boot up my laptop. Alex is used to my writing sprints and eats in silence. After he is done, he grabs his bag from the floor and meanders upstairs. I hear the shower turn on and smile to myself feeling complete. My little family is all here and, for the first time since my parents' accident, I feel truly happy.

∾

Dane

Hot water flows over me as I try to ease some of the tension from my body. Walking away from Emma was difficult and I'm suffering for it, but I don't want our relationship to start off with sex. It's taking all my willpower not to go back over there, but I know it's the right thing. She's not someone to just spend the night with and move on from. She is someone to build a forever with and I don't want our forever to start in a lust filled haze, even though my body hates me right now.

As I crawl into bed, I see the lights are still on in her house. Damn I want to go back so badly. Instead I drop my towel and crawl into bed, closing my eyes and trying to make myself sleep.

Over an hour later I'm still tossing and turning. The need to see her is so strong, I sit up in bed to look out the window. If she is still up I won't be able to resist the temptation any longer. The moonlight is bright and I see that her house is dark. Groaning in disappointment, I lie back down and think of surprising her in the morning. I just want to see her, I want to gauge how she responds to me when we take our hormones out of the mix.

CHAPTER EIGHT

Emma

Persistent knocking at my front door startles me awake from a deep sleep. Squinting at the clock as I roll groggily out of bed, I groan when I see it's only 5:30 a.m.

What. The. Fuck?

Stumbling out of my room, I see Alex is almost at the door looking just as disheveled as I feel.

He opens it as I start making my way carefully down the stairs, knowing me I will slip and tumble if I'm not careful, especially in this state of only partial awareness.

Dane stands on the other side of the door. His face goes from smiling to shock in a split second as Alex greets him sleepily. I've just reached the bottom of the stairs and he looks over at me and then shifts his eyes from Alex to me and back to Alex. Hurt flashes through his eyes before he hardens his face into a look of stony disgust.

"I'm sorry," he chokes out, "I didn't realize you had company." Turning on his heel, he stalks away. I'm full of confusion until I glance over at Alex. He's only wearing boxer briefs and here I am standing at the bottom of the stairs in my sleep shorts and tank top, yeah, that doesn't look good.

Shoving past Alex, I stumble my way onto the porch. "Dane, wait!"

He stops, turning around in the spot, but not moving any closer.

"Well, this is going to be fun," I mutter to myself. Glancing behind me, I see Alex watching us with cautious eye until I shoo him back inside. He rolls his eyes and shuts the door leaving Dane and me outside alone.

Crossing the lawn to where Dane waits, I try to ignore the closed off look on his face.

"That's my *friend*, Alex. He moved in with us when I was twelve, he was wrapping some stuff up at home before moving here because we're family." I know how bad the whole situation looks, but part of me is annoyed at his assumptions. I know we don't truly know each other that well anymore, but I would hope he would realize I wouldn't be kissing him if I was involved with someone else.

A look of understanding crosses his face, and he finally relaxes as he nods. "I wish you would have told me he was coming so I didn't need to find out this way."

His tone is soft, but there is a hint of frustration that raises my hackles.

Crossing my arms, I frown at him. "I didn't realize he was arriving last night; if I knew, I would've told you."

"You've actually never mentioned him to me, I've only heard his name when he called you on your first night, the night you told him you love him," he bites back.

It's too damn early to be arguing on the lawn, but I stand

my ground. "You're right, I don't know why I haven't mentioned him in passing. Yet, you still let me kiss you."

He closes off, looking towards the barn. "Look, I think we both need to take a few breaths, and I have chores to do. Let's talk about this later, because I don't want to argue with you over something so ridiculous."

Sighing, I wrap my arms around my body. It's cool out this early in the morning, and I've only been asleep for maybe three hours, so I agree. Turning on my heel, I head back inside and slowly climb back up the stairs and face plant back into bed.

It's several hours later before I make my way back downstairs. Entering the kitchen, I walk to the fridge and start pulling food out.

"Instead of going next door for breakfast, why don't we stay here and visit?" If I'm being honest with myself, I'm avoiding confrontation with Dane. I can't believe we were going to argue about something so silly.

Alex looks up from his laptop and shakes his head at me. "You two kids didn't work it out this morning?"

I shake my head. "We agreed to talk about it later."

"It's later. You're going to have to face him sometime." Straight to the point is Alex's style with me. We know each other too well to try anything else, so we gave up beating around the bush a long time ago.

"This is why I didn't want to act on how I was feeling. Even after I explained who you were he was still all uptight." I pour us some coffee before starting on putting together breakfast. Talking to Alex always helps me, he is able to bring a different perspective or give me something to think about.

"It was unfortunate timing . . ." He trails off. Well, usually he is helpful. Frowning at him, I start mixing up eggs to make omelets and resist saying something sarcastic. "Why was he so surprised to see me? Surely he had to know I was coming at some point."

Flushing, I avoid his gaze and ignore his question. "You know, I'm a little irritated. Who shows up at five thirty in the Goddamn morning?" Alex just looks at me as I vent. He knows better than to point out where my anger is truly coming from: fear. I can feel it coursing through my veins and I turn my attention to the package of bacon in my hands as I fight back tears.

"You didn't have a nightmare last night." He changes the subject. Arching an eyebrow at him, I decide to let him get away with it because truthfully, I'm grateful.

"They are coming less and less. I thought I would have one, I talked with Lia about the accident and all my struggles, but I think having you home made a difference." I exclude the fact that Dane also played a part when he came to visit and made my toes curl with his kiss.

As we finish washing our breakfast dishes, I remember the plastic eagerly waiting for us. "I have something fun planned for us, but since you're here sooner than expected, you need to help me set up."

My property has the perfect hill for a slip and slide and while we were in town the last time I had bought some plastic so we could have a slip and slide party when Alex arrived. In the back of my mind I also know it will provide me an opportunity to see when Dane comes back from running to the tack shop.

After changing into our swimsuits, I grab some towels and we head outside.

As I finish rolling out the plastic, Alex goes to the side of the house to find a longer hose.

"What are you doing?" I jump as Lia startles me.

"Alex and I are making a slip and slide. You and Ryan should join us."

"Alex? Oh! That's where that truck and trailer came from. He's here early."

"He wanted to surprise me. Arrived last night shortly after Dane left." Blushing, I turn away as I think about the amazing kiss.

"Something happened between you two finally, didn't it?" she smugly asks. Nodding, I straighten out the already perfect plastic.

"We kissed and then he left. But he came by early this morning and Alex answered in his underwear. We got in an argument."

"What all have you told Dane about Alex?"

"I guess I've never really mentioned him to Dane, as he pointed out this morning. He saw him call my first night but other than that the topic hasn't come up. And he hasn't been around when Alex has called. You never filled him in on that?"

"I guess I never really thought it would be necessary and, to be honest, I always wondered if there was something more until you started seeing Johnathan. I can see why he misread the situation. Dane's high school girlfriend was a bit of a slut. It's uncertain if she ever cheated on him, but he is pretty sensitive about feeling like a fool and hasn't really let anyone get close since."

"We will straighten this out, it just got a bit heated this morning." Biting my lip, I stress over how to fix this. Now that I understand why he would have reacted that way, all I can think about is making it right. I don't want him to feel like a fool for kissing me and I definitely don't want him to think I'm purposefully keeping anything from him.

"Well, as fun as this looks, I need to go to work." Lia looks longingly at the plastic now spread out on the ground, before hugging me goodbye. I gaze towards the road, worrying my lip between my teeth as I wonder when Dane will come back. Lia leaves me to my pondering with an empathetic look. "You guys will sort things out."

Alex comes back with the hose as Lia is walking away. Gesturing in her direction he inquires, "Who was that?"

"That was Lia. She can't slip and slide with us but we'll still have fun." Attempting to brighten the mood I steal the hose from Alex and spray him. As he stands there soaking wet, I can't help but burst into laughter. Before I can run away, Alex has wrapped me in his arms and is wrestling the hose away from me. We are laughing and wrestling in the water when Dane drives up and parks in front of the barn. He glances over at us with an unreadable expression before he starts unloading the truck.

I watch as he finishes the task, glances at us one more time, and then heads into the house. Sighing, I run my fingers through my wet hair. "This is not the foot I was hoping the two of you would get started on."

"Why don't you go over there?" Alex asks quietly. He knows I want nothing more than to fix this now, it's always been my way. Once I'm done being angry about something, I want it dealt with and forgotten. Looking down at my bikini clad body and the hose now running water down the slip and slide, I shake my head.

"I do want to finish our discussion and move past it, but I also want us to have our day. Let's enjoy the sun and play on the slip and slide and I will go there after I've cleaned up." Alex shakes his head, but knows it's futile to argue with me.

For the rest of the afternoon we slide and have a water fight. Ryan arrives home from work and we ambush him as he gets out of his truck. Yelling a fake battle cry he grabs the water gun from Alex's hands and chases after me. Throwing myself down the hill, I grin when I hear Ryan say, "Aw, what the hell" and jumps onto the slide after me. We play around for a while longer before calling it a day.

As we clean up I realize the guys haven't had a chance to be introduced so I gesture between them. "Ryan, this is Alex. He has lived with me and my parents since I was fourteen years old." The guys start talking and seem to hit it off.

Excusing myself, I head inside to get cleaned up and mentally prepare myself to sort things out with Dane. Now that I have opened up to the possibility of being more, it terrifies me that maybe we're not as compatible as we had seemed. We're already arguing and we've only kissed once. I wasn't always so fearful of losing people, but having three of the most important people in my life torn away from me has left me damaged. I'm scared to let anyone in for fear of losing them, especially with the issues I'm working through.

As I shower and get dressed, I'm in pep talk mode. Reminding myself of the confident woman I was a year ago I straighten my shoulders and walk over to their house. Ryan and Alex are still talking as Alex feeds the horses and they wave at me as I pass by. Alex gives me an encouraging smile and Ryan winks in the comforting way that only he can.

Taking a deep breath before opening the front door, I slowly walk into the house. I wander throughout trying to find Dane before making my way to his bedroom. Leaning into the door, I hear him moving about inside.

Taking another deep breath, I knock. "Dane?" The movement in the room continues, but I get no answer. "Please open the door so we can finish talking." My voice cracks a bit when there is no movement towards the door.

The realization that he is not going to answer slowly sinks in and tears start to well in my eyes. Waiting a moment longer before I turn and slowly head back down the stairs. Pausing at the front door to look behind me, I feel the weight that's been lifting settle back onto my shoulders when the stairwell remains empty.

I walk blindly home, avoiding Ryan and Alex's gazes in order to maintain my composure as I walk into my house, calling Chloe in with me, and up to my room. Stoically closing the door and crawling into bed with Chloe wrapped in my arms before I let the tears break through. Although I try to tell myself that I know that Dane will come around at some point, he just needs more time to process, my heart still feels as though I have experienced another significant loss and it aches in a way that I haven't felt since coming here. It's with tears in my eyes and my face buried into Chloe's neck that I fall into a restless sleep.

～

Dane

Music pounds through my headphones as I finish another set of pushups. I'm so fucking frustrated with myself, I shouldn't have gotten so riled up this morning, but all I could see was the future I envisioned disappearing.

I can't just fucking sit here and stew. I need to clear my head so I can work this out with her. I'm not good with immediate confrontation, I need to think through all the possible scenarios beforehand so I'm prepared for anything.

Picking up my phone, I dial without thinking and wait for the familiar voice on the other end of the line.

"Hey, man, what's up?" my best friend greets me.

"I need a night out, want to go to Linger tonight?" Jesse has been my best friend since high school and even though life makes it difficult to spend much time together he is still my bro and that will never change.

"I'm surprised you don't want to spend your time figuring out how to trick Emma into going out with you." He laughs, his words meant to be teasing.

"We kind of got in a fight and I just need to clear my head of her."

He agrees, knowing I need a change of pace while I figure my shit out.

Linger Bar and Grill looks like a dive on the outside. The worn cedar siding, blacked out windows and crooked sign ward off people driving by. They're missing out.

Laughter, glasses clinking, and the smell of delicious food assaults all my senses as I walk into the pub. Michael, the owner, did an amazing job when he bought and renovated the building. He intentionally left the outside alone, it keeps the crowd small. The inside though, it could easily become one of the places to go, it's a must see.

The lighting is soft and warm. There are simple wall sconces throughout and then in the center is a unique glass blown chandelier. It's not fancy or large, but the way it reflects light gives the room a subtle shimmer, a magical quality.

The bar is in the center of the room with comfortable wooden stools all the way around. Along the outer wall are cozy booths, some large enough to fit big groups and others more intimate for couples. The kitchen is down the hall to provide optimum space for the customers. This place is a hidden gem and the comfort of being here automatically relaxes me at least a little.

Scanning the room, I see Jesse as he shouts my name and I

meander through the crowd of people to the booth he has snagged us.

"What's up?" Jesse fist bumps me as I take a seat.

"Not much. Needed a night out to clear my head. I don't want to say anything I will regret and I'm still trying to figure out why I'm still so annoyed." Jesse looks at me critically but I scan the crowd and avoid his gaze. Linger is always busy, right from when it opens at four in the afternoon until it closes at three in the morning.

Jesse flags down the server and orders us a couple Big Rock Traditional Ale's.

Taking a large gulp, I savor the flavor in my mouth. "Damn, we brew good beer here." Jesse nods in agreement and we scan the crowd some more. No familiar faces which is unusual.

"So, what's going on with you? How are things at the ranch?"

"We have some foals that have good prospects. I'm trying to find ways to expand, but at the same time things are flowing so smoothly I might just leave it. Other than that, I'm good. What about you?" He nods, the wheels in his head turning. He lets it slide when I don't bring up Emma, but I'm sure the topic will come up again soon.

"I'm tired of working at a desk. I want to be outside, but I want to stick close to home. I feel trapped in so many ways." The unhappiness in Jesse's voice shocks me and the fact I have no idea what is going on in my friend's life makes me feel like shit.

"I had no idea. What a crappy friend I am."

"I hide it well, but I'm exhausted from pretending to be something I'm not." Jesse looks me in the eye and I get the feeling he is talking about more than dissatisfaction at work.

"You don't need to hide, whatever it is you know I have your back. As for the work, I have been tossing around the idea of hiring someone to help me, are you interested? You know the ranch and I know you're a hard worker."

"Seriously? Fuck! That's awesome!" We grin at each other and I realize that this is the first time since I sat down that Jesse has smiled. What the hell is going on? He flags down the server and we order a couple more beers.

"Dane, what are you doing here instead of talking to Emma?" Jesse holds my gaze, unwavering and I groan. I don't want to talk about it.

"I'm processing."

"Bullshit."

"I need to think about what I'm going to say. I don't want to argue with her again, especially over something that now feels so trivial. I guess I just don't understand why she kept Alex a secret from me." It's been weighing on me all afternoon.

"Dude, have you talked to her about me?" Jesse picks up his beer when I look at him and shake my head. He sips at it, watching me, waiting.

"What?"

"Why would she think to mention Alex? He's a part of her life, something that is a constant. She's been back for what, a month? What have you talked about? Have you talked about her life over the past thirteen years?" Jesse's questions all make a lot of sense.

"Crap." Shaking my head, I down the last of my beer. Glancing at my watch, I sigh. "I will wait until tomorrow, at a reasonable hour this time."

"Good. Don't be a pussy."

CHAPTER NINE

Emma

We're singing along to My Fault by Imagine Dragons and I'm laughing at my dad's animated gestures. Looking to my right, I smile at the grin on Dane's face. He hasn't seen my parents in years and he is thoroughly enjoying this visit. He reaches his hand over to squeeze mine and I'm the happiest I can remember being.

I wish everyone was able to come to dinner, but Lia, Ryan, and Alex all had to work. Dad continues to joke around and Mom is smiling at his antics. Mom has never tired of his humor and neither have I. He is one of the funniest people I know and is always coming up with some new joke to tell us. My mom, on the other hand, is soft spoken, kind, gentle, and generous. They complement each other perfectly and I can't believe how lucky I am to have them.

Sighing contentedly, I watch as Dane strokes his thumb over my skin. My mind wanders to the upcoming weekend and all that I have planned for my parents' visit when squealing tires break into my thoughts. Quickly looking to the right, my mother and I scream as a semi-truck comes careening into us . . .

"Emma! Emma! Wake up, you're okay." Alex's calm voice breaks through my screams and I choke awake. Tears are streaming down my face as I turn into him sobbing. Breathing in short abrupt bursts the panic rises and my body shakes with the pain in my heart.

Alex pulls me into his arms and holds me. He is used to this routine and I will never be able to show him how much I appreciate his patience and comfort. Squeezing him hard, my breathing evens out and the tears slowly come to a stop. I pull away and look out my window. It's dark and I have been asleep for several hours. The thought of going to sleep again scares the hell out of me, but it's too early in the morning to get up.

"Will you stay with me?" I whisper. Alex nods and crawls over to the other side of the bed. I remember doing this for him when he first moved in with us. It's come full circle that he is now returning the favor. Just having him next to me will help keep the nightmares away.

Alex falls asleep and I lay there listening to his even breaths. Matching my breathing to his, I try to clear my mind of my nightmare before rolling away from him and dozing off.

Waking up earlier than normal, I quickly feed the horses and jog with them before going into the house. After sleeping like crap, I look like hell. It's amazing what one night of poor sleep will do. The black bags under my eyes are back and there is a droop to my mouth that hasn't been there since I first moved up here.

Coming into the house the smell of bacon makes me smile. Alex had still been asleep when I got up, but he must have crawled out of bed shortly after I did. He knows me so well, understanding that I won't want to go to the Hyatt's for breakfast until Dane and I can work things out on our own. I don't need an audience for that. Besides, after a nightmare I always enjoy pigging out on my favorite comfort foods: bacon and French toast.

My mouth starts watering at the smells that are assaulting me as I walk through the house. I have already texted Lia to let her know I won't be there for breakfast. Her response makes me chuckle.

> Lia: Fine. Tomorrow, I bring out my ropes. Want to hang out later?

> Oh, never mind. I forgot you had plans with Alex. I heart you hard!

> Me: I heart you hard too.

Tossing my phone onto my desk before making my way into the kitchen. I don't bother trying to hide how utterly exhausted I am. Alex looks at me and purses his lips as I sit down at the breakfast bar with a resigned sigh.

Ignoring the look on his face, "I thought we could take Chandler and Serenity out today. It will be good practice for you." I've been attempting to teach Alex to ride for years, but horses have always been more my passion. He enjoys looking after them when I go to signings or I'm sick, but in terms of riding he prefers his feet planted firmly on the ground. He will come around, there is a cowboy in him yet.

"You know I don't need to practice something if I don't intend on doing it frequently, right? However, I will go along just because I love you." Grinning at him as I wolf down my breakfast, I try to think about when Dane usually breaks from working so I can finally talk to him.

Lia's words ring through my head that I will not lose them, no matter what happens with Dane. The tiny, pessimistic voice in the back of my head whispers that I may not lose Lia or

Ryan, but I could potentially lose Dane. I shove those thoughts to the dark corners of my mind where I store all my guilt and worries and give myself a mental shake as I finish eating. Hugging Alex in thanks for breakfast, I throw on my cowboy boots and head out to get the horses ready.

Grinning to myself as I carry Serenity's saddle to the paddock, the excitement that always accompanies any time spent with my horses sets in. I swing the saddle to rest on the rail and turn around to go grab Chandler's equipment, halting when I see Dane coming out of their barn with his horse. Fighting my flight instinct, I start to walk over to him. He looks at me and before I can take ten steps he has swung up into the saddle and taken off at a canter in the opposite direction.

There was a time when that kind of action would just piss me off. Part of that girl still remains as anger floods through my body at how he said we would talk about what happened and is now avoiding me.

Underlying that though, overwhelming it even, is the panic and pain that accompanies any risk of losing someone I care about. In the short few weeks I have been home Dane has become an integral part of my life . . . again.

One kiss was all it took to change that. One kiss was all it took to increase the risk of losing another person from my life. One kiss may be enough to break me.

～

Dane

From the shadow of the barn, I see Emma carrying her saddle to the paddock. She has a smile on her face but unless my eyes are playing tricks on me, the deep purple shadows under her eyes are back. I feel sick to my stomach at how our fight is impacting her and the fact we haven't had time to talk.

Leading Charger out of the barn, Emma's gaze meets mine and it feels like she is stabbing me over and over with that sorrow turned in my direction. She starts to walk towards me, but there is an injured horse that needs my immediate attention. Gritting my teeth, I pull myself into the saddle and take off, the look of hurt on her face following me throughout my ride.

CHAPTER TEN

Emma

Alex comes out of the house and grabs Chandler's equipment off the porch before I have a chance to get there. Carefully schooling my expression into one of calmness, I begin saddling up the horses. Lia's massage therapy has done wonders for Belle and I promise her I will take her out soon.

"Ride Serenity, she knows the property well now and I don't want you to be nervous." Alex typically rides Chandler because he is the bigger horse and they are a better fit, but I want to ensure he knows the lay of the land before I throw Alex up there.

I quickly hop up onto Chandler's back and laugh as Alex awkwardly swings onto Serenity's back. She turns her head to look at him and I'm pretty sure if horses could roll their eyes hers would be rolling.

With an "oof" and some choice words, Alex sits up on Serenity. Turning Chandler away from Alex, I restrain my laughter until a snort sneaks out. Unable to hold it back, I lay on Chandler's neck as I laugh, tears running down my cheeks.

"Oh sure, laugh it up. Not everyone does this every day you know!" He chuckles. The relief in his face at my laughter is evident. Apparently, I didn't hide the shift in my mood from Dane's quick departure as well as I had thought.

Narrowing my eyes a bit, I would be willing to bet he exaggerated his struggle to get me to laugh. He winks at me, confirming my suspicion, and I can't help but grin.

Refocusing my attention on getting ready to ride, I close my eyes and breathe deeply while speaking in a low tone to Chandler. Feeling him underneath me, I clear my mind and focus on our connection.

The connection and feeling a rider has on their horse is crucial. I always go through this ritual whenever I ride because whatever is going on outside has nothing to do with my time with the horses. Chandler takes a deep breath and lowers his head, he can feel the shift in my energy and I know we are ready to go.

Alex and I keep to my ten acres and wind through the paths at a leisurely pace.

"This property is truly beautiful. It must have been terrible leaving it behind."

"At first it was, but then I met you. I always wished to come back here, but in my mind, you were here with me." We smile at each other and I continue leading the way through the trees.

Glancing down, I smile as Chloe walks alongside us. She has been trailing Chandler's heels since the start. Alex always calls her my shadow because she's constantly by my side or within sight. Last night she had slept between Alex and me in an attempt to provide more comfort. Typically Chloe sleeps by the front door, I believe in order to guard me while I am sleeping, however whenever I have a nightmare she will crawl into bed with me.

Between Alex, Chloe, and my horses, the support I have keeps me grounded. When that support expanded to once again include the Hyatts, I couldn't have been happier. Most people wouldn't consider me shy, especially once they know me, but I'm guarded with new relationships. That only increased after my parents passed away, but with the Hyatts I never imagined that I would need to shield myself from any of them.

My heart aches for Dane and the state our friendship is in. I can't even call it a relationship as we only shared one kiss. Allowing myself to open up to the possibility of being more was extremely difficult for me and the pain associated with his withdrawal makes me wonder if it was worth it. My mind battles between two different outcomes.

Eventually we will finally talk it through and he will see that Alex and I are essentially siblings, erasing any doubt he might still carry. When that time comes will he want to rekindle what we started and if he does, should we? Recalling the heat in the kiss and the way I felt makes me wish we could pick up right from that night. The other side of me, the guarded one, says to call it a day and go back to being friends while we still can.

"Earth to Emma . . ." Alex laughs as I come out of my reverie and look back at him. "Uh oh. I know that look. You are overanalyzing things again, aren't you? Wait, I don't even need you to answer that. Let me tell you something, as your best friend and your brother, I'm not going to allow you to think about this. Things will work out however they do and we are just going to go with the flow." I give him a small smile, he is right.

"You're right . . . but . . ."

"Wait! Did you just admit that I'm right? We need to commemorate this moment. Where is a knife? I need to carve that in this tree so we can come here and remember this in the years to come!" Alex keeps going like this and I can't contain my laughter. He has always been so good at shifting a mood.

After his dad left, even with his mother losing her marbles, he stayed positive and such a bright shining star. The best day was when he moved in with us and I knew my best friend was safe. He had nightly nightmares, but I would crawl in bed with him and we would share ghost stories, or make jokes. My parents quit trying to stop us as they quickly realized nothing was going on and gradually Alex's nightmares came to an end. Throughout it all, no one truly knows what he had been through before he moved in with us. He still hasn't fully opened up to me, not because he doesn't trust me, but because he always tries to protect me.

"You know what?" I nudge Chandler into a canter as I see my field up ahead and take off. "Catch me, loser!" Laughing as we shoot off, Alex's cursing fades as we leave him in our dust.

The wind blows my long hair back as we pick up speed. The rush that comes with flying across the landscape, feeling the power of the horse moving underneath me, has no comparison. The worries from the day disperse from my mind as we race over the hill. It's been a long time since I just let Chandler go and pick up speed to however fast he wants. Laughing as we charge across the landscape, my hair whipping out behind me, I feel free.

Knowing Alex will have at most bumped Serenity up to a trot, I reluctantly turn and start to make my way back. As I look towards where I left Alex I'm shocked as I see him and Serenity cantering towards me. Jaw dropping, I watch as they get closer and I see the huge grin on Alex's face.

It's been six years since I got my own horses and started

trying to get Alex to ride. He never went above a trot. To see him at a canter and with a smile on his face must signify some weird atmospheric shift. As he comes to a stop alongside us, I look at him and then start scanning the sky.

"What are you looking for?"

"Flying pigs. Because the last time I tried to get you to go faster than a trot your exact words were, when pigs fly."

"She kind of just took off before I could rein her in and it was fun. What can I say, you were right. I didn't really think about how thrilling it would be."

Staring at him, I'm at a loss for words. Shaking my head, I grin at Alex and start planning all the different things we can do. "We're going to have so much fun! I have so much to teach you, but for now we should head back. You're going to be sore tomorrow."

We spend the rest of the day working. Alex runs his own online graphic business and has a backlog of things he needs to work on. He looks after all my digital promotions. Teasers, website, banners, trailers, you name it and he can do it.

The fact that both of us work from home has been a blessing and a curse. Times like today we are both in the zone and really productive. I will read bits of my book to him and he will get my opinion on a website or promotion he is working on. Other times all we do is distract each other. This one time we had an all-out food fight when I began throwing popcorn at him during a writing block. It was glorious, until we had to clean it up.

Thinking of this, I pick up some popcorn and start throwing the kernels at him.

"Hey! Remember what happened last time?" Laughing we both hold our hands up in surrender and go back to work.

As I'm writing, my thoughts wander back to the dark recesses of my mind and pull out all my worries about Dane.

The words flowing from my fingertips reflect the pain and confusion I feel over how to proceed. I wasn't worried that morning, we both needed time to cool down, but we're now on day two of no contact. The more time that passes, the more it hurts. This new novel is a reflection of everything I keep locked inside. It may never get published but I'm hoping it helps me release everything I'm holding onto.

Since being back home I have come to realize how much I need to deal with my grief. The words flow from my fingers and it's therapeutic in a heartbreaking way.

In order to address my loss, I first needed to deal with the guilt at being the cause of the loss . . .

I abruptly stop as those words flow from my fingertips.

Memories of that evening flood my senses. My little commuter car had broken down once again and I called my parents. They'd been offering their car for months because they felt mine wasn't safe, but I hadn't taken them up on their offer, saying I would buy a new one soon.

It was on their way to get me that the semi-truck smashed into them. It's always been at the forefront of my mind that it's my fault they died, but I've never put voice to those thoughts and writing it out makes it seem more real.

Glancing sideways at Alex, I wipe the tears forming in my eyes. Because of my stupid need to keep my car instead of using their car, I caused them to be away from home when they should have been crawling into bed. If it wasn't for me, they would be alive.

No longer wanting to see the words, I shut my laptop and turn on the TV. A reality show is on and I decide to leave it. Alex gives me a surprised look, but I pointedly keep my face turned towards the screen as they hold some kind of vote about who gets eliminated.

As the show ends, I turn as Alex gets up and groans when

his back cracks. Smiling at him as he leans down to hug me, I feel his warmth right to my center and the sorrow eases, I'm so glad to have him in my life.

"I'm done for the night, Em. Love you." Alex kisses my forehead.

"Love you too."

Sitting there alone I scan the channels until I find a *Friends* marathon. My mind is not really on the show, but at least my senses aren't being flooded with the feelings surrounding the Dane situation or, even worse, thinking to myself about the fact that my parents died because of me.

Four hours and countless *Friends* episodes later, I finally turn off the TV when I doze off and fall off the couch. Reluctantly, slowly, I climb up the stairs and crawl into bed. Staring at the ceiling, I fight my eyes as they droop, heavy with sleep, for as long as I can, but inevitably I fall asleep.

Dane

It takes a couple of hours to get the mare stable, but when I'm finally happy with her state, I ride Charger back to the house hoping to catch Emma before I need to head back out to complete my chores. When I get home, I ride right over to her house instead of stopping at the barn. Belle stands alone in the paddock and I realize they went for a ride so I won't be able to see her until later.

It's late by the time I get home. There was another broken fence to repair on top of everything else on my to do list for the day. The mare is still recovering, so I brought her back to the barn with me. By the time she's settled in, I'm exhausted.

I go straight to my room, ignoring Lia and Ryan as they both try and find out why I haven't talked to Emma yet, because I don't feel bad enough. Deep inside, I know I could've probably make time, but I'm still a little hurt that she didn't talk to me about Alex. It's stupid, but who said that human nature is always reasonable.

Shutting my door behind me, I strip out of my clothes and turn on the shower. Covered in dirt, and feeling numb from pushing myself today, I crawl under the stream of hot water.

Seeing him open the door and thinking that I misunderstood the tension building between Emma and I, honestly never in my life have I felt so torn up. A stampede of horses trampling me would have been preferred to that feeling. The feeling of disappointment and betrayal. Even though I know it's nothing, a hint of that feeling lingers. Emma surrounds me in everything. Her photos are throughout our house and she has taken over my dreams.

The way her lips felt on mine and the memory of her soft moans is torture, my body reacts even just thinking about her legs wrapped around my waist, her body pushing into mine.

My hands fist in my hair as I try to push her from my mind, but it doesn't work. She's always fucking there. Always out of reach. This is what it would be like if I lost her. And my head is warring with my heart about the risk.

The water turns cold and the reality of time slipping away as I drown in my thoughts, I shove the tap in and dry off vigorously. My cock is hard from thinking about her and the urge to give in to the need for release is strong.

"Get down!" I yelled at my dick. I'm going crazy.

Throwing on my sweats, I lay in bed and put my earbuds in. Cranking it loud, I drown out my thoughts with Memphis May Fire's album *Challenger*. Listening to the songs and memorizing the lyrics, I argue with myself over letting myself imagine life without her. I'm totally overreacting, tomorrow I will go over there first thing and we will talk. More than enough time has passed.

A pounding noise wakes me and I jump out of bed startled. It's dark outside and as my brain slowly wakes up I realize I just slept the evening away. The pounding continues and I realize it's at the front door so I rush out of my room and down the stairs as Lia opens the door.

Alex stands at my door in jeans that are unbuttoned. Does the guy not know how to put fucking clothes on?

He looks at Lia and the murderous gaze on his face disappears as she stands silent in the doorway. My body starts shaking as he blatantly checks her out in front of me. Closing the distance between us, I cross my arms.

"Can we fucking help you?" I snap at him. It's the middle of the night and if I'm honest with myself, I'm still jealous over his relationship with Emma.

His rips his gaze away from my sister and if I was easily intimidated, the expression on his face would scare me. Good thing I'm not.

"You!" He shakes his finger at me and carefully steps past Lia. "You need to come with me. I need to show you something."

"Why would I go anywhere with you?" Planting my feet, I cross my arms in challenge. I feel Ryan come to stand behind me.

"You are going to come with me because you and Emma need to finally have that discussion you were supposed to have two days ago. I'm tired of it impacting someone I love the way it is. You need to see what you're doing to her." I'm confused about what he is referring to by how I'm impacting Emma, but the second he utters the word love I feel that burning jealously flare up. It's unreasonable, but he got the years I lost.

"Can't it wait until morning? I was planning on stopping by then. I'm sure Emma doesn't want to discuss this in the middle of the night."

"No. So, we can do this the easy way or the hard way. It's your choice." I'm about to shove him out the door when I hear Ryan's voice over the roar of rage in my ears.

"Go with him, Dane. It's not up for discussion." Hurt floods through me as Ryan and Lia stand together, pointing out the door. Lia's eyes keep flickering to the guy standing there. No way in hell is that happening. I'm still not certain I like this guy.

Shoving my feet into my boots, I follow Alex across the yard. Anger radiates off him as he glances back to make sure I'm there.

He opens the door and filtered screams sound from upstairs. Abruptly stopping, shock fills me and I look to Alex.

"What the fuck?"

Alex explodes at my question and I can't even keep up with the string of curses and ranting he is directing at me. My feet propel me to follow him up the stairs, towards the screams that rip my heart out chunk by chunk.

"You both agreed to talk this through once you've calmed down. How long do you need? She tried to talk to you and you ride away without even a wave. Over what? Because I answered the door in my underwear? I'm basically her fucking brother and this is my home. Now, I'm going to give you the benefit of the doubt because I understand she didn't really talk about me, but dude, you live within eyesight. You know she lost her entire family, and then you withdraw? That basically thrust her back into her nightmare. You need to fucking fix this and in the future, maybe give yourself an hour or two if you need time to think. If you hurt her, your face won't be nearly so pretty."

Shit. I've been such an ass. He's right, because the more time that's passed the more I've doubted my common sense. I need to fix this.

CHAPTER ELEVEN

Emma

We're singing along to My Fault by Imagine Dragons and I'm laughing at my dad's animated gestures. Smiling as I look to my right, I falter at the hostility on Dane's face. I reach over to try to communicate with him but he turns away from me. I force a smile on my face as Dad continues to joke around and Mom is smiling at his antics, both oblivious to the tension in the back seat.

Mom has never tired of Dad's humor and neither have I. He is one of the funniest people I know and is always coming up with some new joke to tell us. Despite this, I'm forcing my laughs rather than truly enjoying his jokes.

Sighing with regret that I'm not enjoying their visit more, I turn to look out the window. My mind wanders between the upcoming weekend and all that I have planned for my parents' visit and ways to try to sort things out with Dane. He has been so distant and I can't stand it. Squealing tires break into my thoughts. Quickly looking to the right, my mother and I scream as a semi-truck comes careening into us . . .

"No!" Sobbing, I rouse a little from the dream as I scream at the scene in my head. It continues to play over and over as I'm trapped in a half dream state.

"Enough is fucking enough!" Faintly I hear Alex's voice break through my cries as he storms downstairs and slams the front door. Unable to pull myself from the nightmare I'm stuck in, my consciousness turns back inward.

I gaze on from beside the car as the firemen try to put the fire out. I'm screaming at them to save my parents and Dane but they ignore me. I can still hear their screams and see the fear in their eyes. I didn't even get to tell them I loved them . . .

Raised voices and inhuman cries break through the dream. Chloe is whining at my door but I don't have the strength to get up and let her in. Curling in on myself I try to distinguish between reality and dream. The horrifying screams scare me and I realize they are coming from me, but I can't stop them.

"You have no fucking idea what this immature avoidance bullshit is doing to her. Do you hear that, you asshole?" Alex's rant and Dane's muffled response somehow breaks through to me before I'm sucked back into my never-ending nightmare.

I look to my side and see Dane standing next to me. I don't know how he got out of the car but he is right there. Reaching for him my hand drops as he looks at me in disgust and walks away.

"Oh my God."

"Get your head out of your ass, and deal with this. Now. I'm going back to bed. She's worth it man, but you need to decide if you are going to put in the work." Their voices make their way into the background of my semiconscious state, I try to tune into them rather than the pictures in my mind but I'm too far gone.

I can't chase after Dane with my parents still in the car and it feels like a part of me is being torn out. Returning to screaming for my parents, I fall to the ground as they quit trying to put out the flames and move to containing them instead. Sobs wrack my body until I can't breathe and everything goes black.

Hands grip my shoulders as I shake and cry. Shoving the hands off my shoulders, I bolt to a sitting position. I can't see who is in my room with me, my eyes are swollen with tears and everything is a blur.

Gasping for air, I swing my legs over the side of the bed and rest my head between my knees. This is the worst dream I've had since moving back home and my lungs feel like they are collapsing with the effort to get enough oxygen. My body hurts with how hard I'm crying and my stomach lurches with the need to stop the images.

I'm on my feet as my stomach roils and race blindly to my bathroom, making it in time as I begin heaving. Hands gently gather my hair from my face and rub my back as my stomach empties. When I'm sure I am done, I slowly turn expecting to see Alex.

Dane's bright green eyes stare back at me and I vaguely recall hearing his voice in my dream. Dropping my head, I brush past him to the sink. Gripping the sides of the sink, I breathe deeply before lifting my face to examine myself in the mirror.

A stranger stares back at me. Green eyes dull and red, face splotchy from crying, hair tangled; the face that stares back at me is the broken girl I thought was starting to go away. Loading up my toothbrush, I finally address Dane. "What are you doing here?" I'm weary from my dream and honestly, the thought of addressing what happened only exhausts me further. He needs to leave so I can recuperate my mind and body. We can have our chat tomorrow.

"Alex came and got me."

"He shouldn't have. I want you to go home." Turning away from him, I quickly brush my teeth and wash my face. When I'm done, he's still standing in my bathroom so I walk to my bedroom door and then crawl back into bed facing away from him.

Chloe jumps in and lays against my stomach. Burying my face into her neck, I listen for Dane to leave. When my bed shifts as he sits next to me, I sigh in exasperation. Try talking to the man for two days, nothing. Tell him to go away and he won't leave.

"Seriously, Dane . . . I can't do this right now. Please go away." I hate that he's seeing me like this, so weak. I hate showing how pitiful I truly am, how even the smallest things can set off my nightmares.

"No. We don't need to talk, we can do that later, but I'm not leaving."

Sitting up, tears filling my eyes, "Why? Why won't you leave? I don't want you here. I don't need anyone else. I can take care of myself. Besides, if I do need someone, I have Alex." Dane flinches at the mention of Alex and I wonder what happened when they talked. "Out of everyone, he is the one who has never left. They were essentially his parents too, go get him. Don't bother yourself by being here, wasting your time."

"You're not a waste of my time, Emma. I'm not leaving." Pain fills his eyes and despite the hurt and need I had felt to fix things, in this moment I can't bring myself to care. Everything hurts too much right now.

Throwing myself down, I know there is no point in arguing with him. He has his mind set and I'm not going to be able to change it. Closing my eyes and breathing in Chloe's comforting scent, I jump when his hands tentatively start rubbing circles on my back. Stiffening against his touch, my body battles with what my heart wants and my horror at him witnessing this vulnerability. I want him to see the woman he thinks I am, not what I've become.

Slowly I relax into his touch, I'm still conflicted, but as usual my heart has won this battle. I'm too exhausted to fight anymore anyways. Dane breathes out a sigh and slowly gets himself settled next to me. He's clearly trying to give me space as the only part of him touching me is his hands. Gradually I start to drift out again, lulled into sleep by the consistent rhythm of his hands.

Sweat drips down my back and my face is pressed into the crook of a neck. Freezing, I slowly lean my head back and look at who I've plastered myself against. My eyes slowly take in a chiseled jaw with the right amount of scruff, leaning back a little further I take in the rest of Dane's sleeping face.

He looks so relaxed and he is as wrapped around me as I am him. My leg is tucked between his and I'm engulfed tightly in his arms. No wonder I'm so damn hot, but it also feels right and that frightens me. The past couple of days have been challenging and that's only after a month of him being back in my life and one kiss. I can't imagine how I would break if we went further and it didn't last.

After assessing how tangled we are, I realize I cannot remove myself without waking him up. My body and my heart are at war with my mind and as my eyes droop heavy with sleep, I suspect I know which is going to win.

Light streams through the window and I bury my face into my pillow. It's time to talk to Dane, and seeing as he's in my bed there's no time to prepare. Cautiously, I turn around only to see the spot he had occupied early this morning is empty. Glancing at the clock, I'm surprised to see it's only seven in the morning.

I roll out of bed and pad slowly to my window. As I look down, my eyes are drawn to the tree in front of my porch. Dane sits on the grass in front of my house, lost in thought. I'm not sure what time he left my room this morning, but I know it's time to face him. Straightening my shoulders, I take a deep breath as I turn away from the window. Here I go.

~

Dane

I'm a colossal jackass.

I've been sitting outside Emma's house for forty-five minutes and all I can think is how much of a dick I've been to someone I tell myself I love. I could've made time to talk to her, but I got scared when I realized the potential she has to hurt me.

When Ryan came out and saw me sitting on the grass, the look of self-loathing on my face he told me to stay and that he would look after the chores until I talked to Emma. The disappointment I could sense underlying his words adds to the ways in which I've fucked up.

Thinking back to last night, I shudder at the memory of the screams coming from Emma. The pain radiating from her will haunt my dreams, especially knowing I brought them back. Then to be turned away by her, the pain and exhaustion in her eyes. It was a sword to the gut. Hasn't she gone through enough? I'm a grown ass man and I behaved like a child.

I hear her front door shut softly and prepare myself to be told to go to hell. I prepare myself to see her close herself off from me, because I've shown her that I have the potential to let her down. And I prepare myself to fight for her.

Emma pads slowly to me and sits next to me. That's a good sign.

She's worth it and I'm going to fix this.

CHAPTER TWELVE

Emma

Quietly opening my front door, I pause to examine Dane. He is facing away from my house towards the horses, elbow resting on his knee and hand gripping his head. Seeing someone as confidant as Dane looking so defeated brings a flood of emotions to the surface. In the light of early morning, everything that has happened just makes me realize that the way Dane makes me feel is worth fighting for. Somewhere inside is the strength to fight and I'm going to be strong. I want to be strong.

Shutting the door, I walk over and sit beside him. He runs his hand through his hair and looks over at me. Examining the look of remorse on his face makes my heart ache. His eyes look sad and his normal smirk is missing.

Dane always looks a little mischievous, like he's planning something, and to see it missing feels wrong. Gazing into his eyes I read the emotions flickering across them. Regret. Anger. Sadness. I'm positive the same emotions are being reflected back at him. Dane sighs while rubbing his hands down his face. Turning towards me, he brings his hand up and cups my cheek.

"I'm so sorry, Em." Pressing his finger to my lips when I go to say something, he shakes his head. "No, let me finish. When Alex opened the door, I was jealous. I knew you were talking to a guy, I saw Alex call you your first night here and I still kissed you. If I was so worried about it, I should have clarified first. Then when I realized my mistake, I was embarrassed. It hurt for us to fight so I needed to clear my head. I promised you we would talk and then I didn't make the time to do it. It's hard, knowing I don't know you as well as I want to, but that's no reason to behave the way I have been.

"I also want to make sure you know that I wasn't ignoring you the other day, I had a sick horse to tend to. I should have waited and told you. I understand if you want to take a step back and re-evaluate the progression of this."

Pulling his hand away from me, he runs his palms over his knees and droops his head. Heart pounding, I dig deep to find some of the remains of the person I once was. I've spent too much time not trying since Mom and Dad died, too much time letting their death sit on my shoulders and control my life.

Thinking of them and Grandpa looking down on me fills me with shame. I wish I could talk to Mom, no twenty-three year old should be missing that connection. The thought of Mom and Dad watching me, seeing how I've spent the time since they passed, fills me with a desire to try harder. These half-assed attempts are not enough and I can imagine what they would be saying.

Mom was always a romantic and she would tell me to take

a leap, she always encouraged me not to let fear stand in my way. Just like she did when I started writing and wanted to finish University in an accelerated program. She told me nothing in life comes easily, at least nothing worthwhile. Mom told me that it would be a long, hard, and emotional journey, I would have to make sacrifices and would change immensely because of those sacrifices.

She also told me that if there was anyone who could do it, it was me. Her words resonate through me as I think back to that conversation. Taking my silence as confirmation that I want to step back, Dane sighs and starts to push off the ground. My hand darts out to rest on his forearm, stopping him from standing, as I finally do something to be proud of. For only the second time in the better part of a year, I'm going to do more than blindly walk through life. I'm going to let go of my fear and live.

"I don't want to take a step back. I understand how it looked. I could have come to you, but I was scared. I guess we should thank Alex for getting fed up. If you think about it, we hardly know each other anymore. It's been thirteen years, Dane. We've both changed. I want to get to know you again." Dane's eyes light up and he smiles at me, pulling me into his arms for a hug. Exhaling softly, I settle into his embrace and enjoy the warmth that runs through my body.

Burying my face into his neck, I hold back a grin when he groans at my breath on the sensitive spot by his ear. "We have a lot of catching up to do." He says gruffly.

"Thirteen years' worth." I grin.

"Let's get started then." He pulls me to my feet and into my house. Heart racing, my libido is disappointed when he pulls me through the house to my living room. He sits on the couch and pulls me down in front of him. Frowning as he ponders our position, he positions my legs on either side of his hips so we're facing each other. He moves his legs so they are the same and smirks at me when he is satisfied. Chuckling, I shake my head and wait to see where he is going with this.

Reaching out he tucks a strand of hair behind my ear and takes a deep breath, I brace myself for what is to come because his look screams mischief.

"What's your favorite color?" he asks, eyes twinkling.

Gaping at him before bursting out laughing. "That was what this whole preamble was about? You want to know my favorite color?"

"We're getting to know each other."

Shaking my head at him, I respond," My favorite color is turquoise."

"What's your favorite book?"

"I can't choose a favorite book! That's like asking a parent to choose a favorite child."

"I'm my parents' favorite." He smirks at me and I roll my eyes.

"My current favorite would have to be . . ." I think on it. It's not an easy decision and changes day to day. "The Marked Men series by Jay Crownover. Don't ask me which book in the series is my favorite, because I'm undecided." He laughs at me.

"I didn't realize that one would be so difficult." Stroking his chin, he looks at me pondering his next question.

Jumping in, I cut him off as he starts to ask another. "Hang on! You need to answer some too. This isn't going to be one-sided! What's your favorite color?" I start him off easy.

"I'm partial to a dark green. Like when you're in the darkest part of the forest with only a few rays of sun to light your surroundings." Nodding in agreement, I picture the land that surrounds us and the peace it brings. Yes, that color and its significance is one of my favorites too.

"Have you read my books?" I grin at him. I'm sure he probably hasn't. Not many men enjoy romance novels.

"I have, and I'm eagerly waiting for the last book to come out. Whenever Lia was done reading your latest novel, I would always borrow it from her." Speechless at his admission, I smile shyly.

"So, you liked them?"

"Liked them? I loved them! Who knew you were so funny?" Laughing when I smack him.

"I have my moments."

"You're great with physical comedy. I particularly enjoyed your water trough bit."

"That was humiliating." Burying my face into my hands as I feel a blush spread through my cheeks.

He pulls my hands away, "It was cute. Besides, you looked sexy standing there all wet." He smirks at me as I blush even more.

"My turn for a question. When did you meet Alex?"

The mention of Alex has me wondering where he is, but I shake it off.

"Alex and I met just under a year after we moved. He and his parents lived next door. We didn't bond right away, his dad was resistant to him coming over, but we soon became inseparable. I think Dad and his mom had known each other before Mom and Dad met. Something like being in a class together.

"Anyway, Alex's dad left them when Alex was fifteen and he moved in with us a year later. I was fourteen. He's a brother to me in every sense of the word except for genetically. Mom and Dad treated him like a son and he's been my rock for as long as he has been in my life. I was his too." The look of shame fills Dane's eyes again. "Dane, don't. You didn't know and Lia said she had never really mentioned Alex to you. Let's just move on from it."

"I'm still sorry. Lia told you what happened with Natalie. I think I was just shocked. My mind shut down and I didn't want to say or do something in anger that I would regret." Moving forward so I'm straddling his hips, I press my lips to his.

"Stop." The kiss is only meant to get him to quit dwelling on something we can't change, but my body has been craving his and desire is distracting me from our game.

Running my hands up his arms, I moan and press my lips more firmly onto his. He lets me set the pace for the kiss, it's light and exploratory, but when I push my tongue into his mouth he takes over.

Flipping me onto my back, he grabs my hands in his and pins them over my head. His grip is firm, but gentle, and drives me crazy. Moaning as he grinds his hips into mine, I relish in the minty flavor of his mouth. He deepens the kiss and rests his body over mine, allowing me to feel his presence, but not crushing me.

Rolling my hips into his, I can feel his cock straining against the zipper of his jeans. Trying to pull one of my hands from his grip, I groan in frustration when he firmly holds them in place. Dane chuckles at my irritation. Moving his lips from mine, he trails a blazing path of kisses to my ear and nips the lobe before whispering, "Not yet."

The man's control is infuriating. His kisses drive me wild and I don't want him to show such restraint, but I know this won't be going any further if he maintains control.

He starts to pull away and I wrap my legs around his waist. I'm not ready for this to end. He gave me a tease of a taste the last time and I'm not willing to let him this time. Something in me shifted today and I'm feeling stronger than I have since my parents died bringing my world crashing down.

Using the strength in my legs I pull his hips down until

they are flush with mine. Running my tongue along his jaw, nibbling here and there, I make my way up to his ear.

"We'll see."

I continue to nip and tease him, grinding my hips against his and I feel his resolve waver. Grinning victoriously when he lets my hands go, I start to run them down his sides to the bottom of his shirt. Mistaking the release of my hands as surrender, I loosen the hold of my legs. Dane looks into my eyes, smirks, and pulls away.

Burying my face into the pillow on the couch, I scream in frustration.

"You're such a tease!" I glare at him. He pulls me in for a kiss and grins at me.

"We have chores to do." With that, I'm pulled to my feet and towards the door. Looking at the clock, I sigh and realize he is right. The horses will be hungry.

Once on the porch Dane kisses me lightly on the lips.

"I have a lot of work to do around the ranch, but I'll see you later." Watching him walk away does nothing to calm my libido. Sighing, I walk in a daze over to the horses and wonder how I'm going to make the day go by quickly.

~

Dane

Riding through the property once the remainder of the chores are complete, I decide to pay a visit to my old treehouse and hang out for a bit. Resisting being physical with Emma is challenging, but I don't want to rush her, not that she seems to be hesitant. The fact that she forgave me so readily was shocking and getting to know her again has been pleasant and surprising.

Charger and I arrive at the treehouse and I release him into the small pen that still stands in the trees, allowing him a rest and time to graze. Checking the ladder, I'm impressed to see it's sturdy and I climb up it, crawling in through the small door. Considering it has been years since I came here, it's in remarkably good condition.

Settling in, I can't help but pull my phone out and text Emma. We finally exchanged phone numbers when we parted this morning and we've been texting on and off all day.

> Me: Favorite game?

Her response comes quickly and it makes me smile. Almost as though she was waiting for me.

> Emma: Cards Against Humanity.

> Me: I've never played before.

> Emma: What? You've got to be joking! We're going to have a game night and play Cards Against Humanity.

> What's your favorite song?

> Me: Radioactive by Imagine Dragons.

> Favorite slow song?

> Emma: I love that song. Imagine Dragons is one of my favorite bands.

> Favorite slow song . . . probably Beside You by Marianas Trench.

Me: Downloading.

I find it in iTunes and download the song. As I impatiently wait for it to finish I try to think of other questions to ask. My phone dings as a text comes in and I eagerly check it to see what question she asks.

Jesse: Notice put in. I can start in a couple of weeks.

Me: That's good news! I want to start clearing some trees and could use the help.

Smiling, I'm glad I could help ease some of Jesse's stress. He seemed off the other night and maybe by spending more time with him I can get him to tell me what's going on. The song finishes downloading so I lay down, turn it on and close my eyes. It finishes and I play it again, the lyrics resonate within me and I love it.

Me: Great song!

Emma doesn't respond right away and curiosity gets the best of me. I need to see what she's doing.

It takes no time to come up to the back of the barn and put Charger in his pen. Walking through the barn, I see Emma is riding with Alex. Despite knowing he is like her brother, jealousy is still at the forefront as I watch them together. I need to make an effort to get to know him and hopefully he won't hate me since I plan on being Emma's forever.

My feet start moving me towards her and I watch as she talks and laughs with Alex. Their interactions are so similar to the way siblings act, remorse fills me as I realize the time I missed out on and the damage to our relationship with someone she considers family. Whatever price I have to pay for my stupidity, I'm willing to pay it.

Stopping to stand at the fence, I watch Emma as she rides Belle. Together they are beautiful to watch. She is very focused and doesn't see me standing there.

Impatiently, I wait for her to see me, I've finally thought of my next question.

CHAPTER THIRTEEN

Emma

"Alex! Remember to align your body in the saddle. You want to sit up straight, but be relaxed."

"I know! I'm trying to remember everything, but it's a lot!"

"You're doing great. I'll make a cowboy of you yet!" He nudges Chandler into a trot, and works on posting correctly. Alex is a natural. He says it's from watching me ride all these years. I told him to stop sucking up. Just watching him ride has me itching to get in the saddle, but I want to give Serenity the day off. Belle has been sound since Lia started working on her three days a week. Glancing at Alex I determine it's okay to saddle up Belle and join him for the last bit of his lesson.

Walking her into the ring, I quickly get her ready.

"He's doing remarkably well considering he hasn't put in much time." Turning at the sound of Lia's voice, I grin as she watches him. I see interest in how she tracks him and when she sees me watching her, she carefully tries to hide it, I know better than to say anything.

"Yeah, once he let Serenity go the other day, he realized how much fun it can be. He's a natural." Swinging up onto Belle, I warm her up and go through the stretches.

"The massage therapy is working wonders on Belle! I wish you would let me pay you."

"Psh, no. It's my pleasure." Lia watches Belle warm up before returning her gaze back to Alex. Her dark brown hair flows down her shoulders indicating she has the day off. She's still in her jeans, tank top and boots though. It's no wonder we get along so well. We've both been raised in the barn, enjoying time outdoors rather than playing dress up inside. Although we both know how to clean up well when we want to.

"Anyway, I came by to see if we could do girls night this weekend. I have a feeling we will have much to catch up on by then." She winks at me. Grinning back at her happily, I shrug my shoulders.

"Absolutely. I will kick Alex to his room and we can veg out." She smiles at me, glances back at Alex, before heading towards her house, waving over her shoulder. "Make sure you're at breakfast tomorrow! I don't plan on being lenient any longer." Laughing at her, I kick Belle into a quick walk and make my way towards Alex. He is staring after Lia, a pensive look on his face.

"Like what you see?" He turns to me and grins when he sees the smile on my face. Rather than answering me, he starts loping with Chandler and I quickly follow suit.

Alex has never been one to talk much about the women he sees or takes interest in. He also has never committed to one woman for any length of time. Lynn was the only woman who lasted longer than six months and she ruined that with her jealousy towards me. He's never said it aloud, but I think he worries that he will turn out like his father.

Alex admitted to me after he had moved in that his father was never faithful to his mother and he left her to go start a new family with the woman he had been seeing since Alex was eight years old. He hadn't been the warmest man to start with, but after we had moved in next door, he became even colder. Alex has been skittish of committing to anyone, never opening up about his history, as though it makes him tainted or unworthy. Shaking my head, I know one day someone special will show him how amazing he is.

"Let's cool him down. You're doing great, Alex."

Alex grins at me and slows Chandler to a walk. "How did I not realize how fun and therapeutic this is until now?"

"Because you're so damn stubborn!" I tease. Laughing, he nods in agreement. We both get so stubborn when we set our minds to something. It's been purely coincidental that we usually agree and therefore have never gotten into a fight.

Alex hops off Chandler and walks him around. Turning my attention to Belle, I lean down to stroke her neck, whispering lovingly to her.

Nudging her into a trot, I relish in the smoothness of her gait. Lia truly has worked miracles since starting the massage therapy treatment on her. She feels better than she has in years. I'm so focused on Belle that I don't notice Dane at the fence until I hear him clear his throat. Smiling, I walk Belle over to him. He leans against the fence, dirt and sweat showing how hard he has worked in the few hours since I've seen him.

Dane grins up at me. "Favorite dessert?"

This random game of twenty questions has been enjoyable and I keep wracking my brain for things to ask. "Raspberry swirl chocolate cheesecake, which you should know." This has been my favorite dessert since I was a child, but I guess it's not fair to assume things are still the same.

Nodding, he starts to walk away. Shaking my head, I call after him, "You came all the way over here for one question?"

"For now. I have to get back to work. I have some paperwork to do, my new ranch hand is starting in a couple of weeks." Smirking at me, he walks backwards towards the house.

"Wait! I get a question!" He saunters back to the fence and looks up at me expectantly. "What's your favorite movie?"

"Hmmm. Comedy, *Without A Paddle*. Action, *The Bourne Series*." He winks, then turns to walk away, typing on his phone. "Oh, you may want to check your phone." With that, he walks to his house, my eyes glued to his perfect ass until he disappears in the door. What a tease. Dismounting from Belle, I pull my phone from my bra and slide my finger across the screen. Jaw dropping, I lean into Belle and grip the saddle horn as I read his text.

> Dane: Favorite sexual position?

When I'm finally able to close my mouth, I type back and hit send before I can second guess myself.

> Me: You're just going to have to figure that out yourself.

> Dane: Challenge accepted.

Butterflies fill my gut at the thought of what that entails and I squeeze my legs to try and contain the ache in my core.

"Why so flushed?" Alex's voice makes me jump and I tuck my phone back into my bra preventing him from reading over my shoulder. He laughs and shakes his head as he pulls the saddle off Chandler. "I'm glad you talked things out. I guess this means I should try to talk to the guy aside from yelling at him and threatening him?"

"We all make mistakes. I think you two will get along. Let's not dwell." He walks over and hugs me before lifting both saddles and carrying them to the tack room alongside the house.

~

Dane

"You look better than you did this morning." Ryan sits down in one of the chairs in my office, looking at me as I work on catching up the books, Lia is sprawled in the other one, nose buried in a book.

"Yeah, it was an eye-opening evening and morning." I know my siblings aren't impressed with me and neither would my parents be if they knew how I behaved. I'm grateful they're on holiday so I only need to deal with Lia and Ryan.

"Serves you right. I can't believe you let days go by without talking to her. Or me for that matter, I would have told you if she wasn't available." Lia has been shooting daggers at me since I came into the house, following me around to remind me of how I've disappointed her. Sighing, I set my pen down and look at them both.

"Hindsight is twenty-twenty. I know I fucked up, and I'm sorry for my behavior. Emma and I have sorted it out, can we please move on?" They both nod and I grin at them. "I hired Jesse as a ranch hand. He seems really unhappy, I'm hoping if he is happier at work the rest will get better too."

"Fantastic, we needed someone and that means I can book

more clients, I've had to turn people away my schedule is so packed." Ryan pushes out of the chair and walks out the door.

I check my phone and sigh when there is no text back from Emma. Her response had been flirty, but I can't help but worry that as the day progresses she will pull away from me.

"She's writing right now." Lia looks up from her book.

"Oh. That's good." My gut still has a sinking feeling and it's all I can do to not go over there.

"Finish what you're doing and go surprise her. I know you want to see her. If you like I can get Alex out of the house." She smiles at me and I know I'm forgiven for my behavior.

"Should I be giving him the big brother talk?"

"I'm pretty sure he's older than you. And no, I'm not looking for a relationship. You know that."

"You need to move on at some point."

"I will, nothing wrong with enjoying my freedom. I'll head over there at six and take Alex out. We can go to Linger. That will give you some time." Closing her book, she looks at the clock on the wall and leaves the room.

Quickly finishing what I was working on, I run upstairs to my bathroom to get ready. It's time to start my challenge.

CHAPTER FOURTEEN

Emma

Creases cross my forehead as I type furiously on my keyboard. The words are flowing and I'm taking advantage of a quiet afternoon to get some work done.

Alex sits on the opposite end of the couch, our feet tangled in the middle with Chloe sprawled out over our legs as we work with intense focus. Pausing, I read through the last paragraph I wrote to make sure it's moving the direction I want and connects with what I've already written.

I've decided to run with the story that is reminiscent of my experiences this past year and I find it to be cathartic sitting here writing out the battle of emotions that feel ever at war in my mind. Alex has read bits of it as I go and he stated he thinks it's one of the most raw and powerful stories I've ever told. I don't have the courage to tell him I'm not sure I will publish it.

It feels too personal, especially the aspects that align with the shift in my relationship with Dane, but this is one more thing I'm at war with myself over. Sighing, my mind flits through what feels like a never ending internal battle. Now that my brain has had time to think about things it has gone back to the darkness that constantly tries to take over. Despite the determination I felt during the day, as I sit and lose myself in my thoughts I can feel it fading and I'm struggling to pull it back.

"That's a heavy sigh." Alex raises his hazel eyes to meet my gaze. They hold concern and it's one of those times I wish he didn't know me so well.

"I feel like it's a lost cause."

"What is?"

"Me. My emotions. My weakness. The constant fear that I'm still waiting for the other shoe to drop. These things come in three's and I'm waiting for the third and final strike that will break me."

"Johnathan wasn't the third?"

"He was an inevitability. I think he'd just been waiting until I didn't have any fight in me. Besides, we were only together for a few months." Rolling my eyes at the thought of that weak man. Realistically we never would have worked, I had been drawing away from him before shit hit the fan in my life because he had no pull on me. Pre-chaos I had the courage to go for what I wanted and let go of what didn't work. I had never fully let him in because I needed to see if he was worthy, the lack of effort on his part to get to know me was apparent.

Dane on the other hand has been like a high-powered magnet, drawing me towards him in the irresistible manner he has mastered. Our history and his interest in me has permeated the walls I've built and it's terrifying.

"I'm not ready for people to see inside the scary place that is my brain. What if they can't handle it, especially if I don't get better?"

"Emma, every day here is a small battle won. I see more of your old self here than I have in months. You have more life to you. It's a day by day journey, and those people over there, they are in it for the long haul. Let them break down your walls, let HIM break down your walls and you may be surprised at the outcome. Better yet, open the gate and let them in."

"I will try." *I don't know if I can.* Alex looks at me and the empathy that fills his eyes speaks volumes about what he sees in me. Nudging him in the knee with my toe. "What about you? Are you going to open the gate and let anyone in?" He shrugs infuriatingly and grins at me.

"You know me, it's going to have to be someone damn determined to bust her way in for that to happen." Reaching over I squeeze his foot. He and I aren't so different in how closed off we are.

Returning to my laptop I let my mind zone in on my story and lose myself once again. The world quiets and all I hear is the click click click as I type the words that fill my head. It never ceases to amaze me when the words flow. Every time I finish writing a book I always think that it may be the last one. Will the stories run out? I don't know if that will happen but until it does I appreciate my ability to do what I love every day.

This is something I once took for granted. Watching my world crash around me as I lost three of the most important people in my life has changed that. There is nothing that I can take for granted; it could be gone in a second.

Pouring the emotions I feel constantly tug-of-warring inside through my fingertips and onto the keyboard, watching the words flow and not really seeing them. Green eyes fill my mind and my thoughts wander to the man who has managed to chisel away at me. I hear what Alex is saying, open the gate and let him in. Take that leap of faith. Don't take his interest for granted, he may not want to continue to slowly work away at my defenses.

What does it say about me that I want to test him and see if he is willing? When did I transition from the carefree little girl that used to be here to the reserved, guarded, and cautious woman who sits in the living room we used to build forts in? If I'm honest with myself, it was before the accident, but I can't pin point when that change happened.

Pinching the bridge of my nose, I try and shift my thoughts. Today has been a good day, I need to remember that it's okay to try and forget everything else for a while. Live in the moment.

Closing my eyes, I lean into the couch and rest my head. It's time to change things and that is going to start right now. No more dwelling and no more second guesses. It's time to take risks outside of my books, outside of the freedom I feel with my horse. Maybe it's time to take a risk with my heart.

Opening my eyes, I return to my manuscript with new vigor and soon lose myself in the words once again.

"Hey, guys." Startled by Lia's voice, I look up from my laptop to where she is standing in the kitchen. She looks stunning in her cowboy boots, jeans, and a purple V-neck top.

"Hey, Lia. Sorry, I was in the zone." Looking over at Alex, his brows are furrowed as he types. He has no idea that Lia is here, this should be good. I kick him and he looks up at me, glasses askew on his face. "Lia's here."

Alex turns to where I'm looking and waves at Lia, turning slightly back to his computer before doing a double take. Barely suppressing my laughter, I watch the two of them eye each other. If it were possible, I swear sparks would be flying.

"Hey, Alex. I am heading to Linger, a pub not too far from here, and I thought you might like to join me." Lia's voice is strong, but I see the nervousness behind the question.

"Yeah, sounds great. I need to get away from the computer for a bit." Alex shuts his laptop and sets it on the table, placing his glasses on top before standing. "Just give me a minute to change."

Lia takes his place on the couch and pulls my feet into her lap. "How are you?"

"I'm better. I'm glad Dane and I worked through that disaster."

"He should have known better than to let things fester for so long." Lia's voice fills with disgust at her brother. I shut my laptop and set it aside.

"Lia, he reacted as he did because it looked bad. Besides, we both needed to cool down and I could've tried harder to seek him out too. Besides, who am I to judge? I'm allowing my life to fall apart because I've experienced a loss. I've had a lot of time to think and I'm going to try to finally get better. Anyway, let's talk about that later. You look hot! Is this a date?" Waggling my brows at her, I burst into laughter at the horror that fills her face.

"No! Oh shit, do you think he thinks it's a date? I don't date. Ugh." Lia's voice is panicked and it makes me laugh harder.

"I'm sure he knows it's not a date. If you like, I could come along to be certain."

"No! No. It's okay. You stay home and get some writing done. How's the book coming?" She abruptly changes the subject and I wonder why she doesn't want me to come, but her question distracts me and I start squirming.

Looking at her guiltily, she narrows her eyes and crosses her arms.

"I may have started writing something totally different." My grin is sheepish as she sighs in fake disappointment.

"You artists! I never will understand you. I can wait and I'm sure whatever you're writing will be amazing!"

Alex comes back into the room, his dark wash jeans and t-shirt hugging his muscles. He's sliding his wallet into his back pocket, completely unaware about how good he looks. When he smiles at us, Lia gapes a bit before collecting herself.

"Okay, see you later." Hugging her, I wink at Alex and he rolls his eyes.

"Love you both!"

The front door shuts and I grab my laptop and start typing again.

~

Dane

Lia and Alex head down the driveway, taillights barely disappearing before I'm out the door. The door is unlocked and I walk in; Emma has scolded me for knocking one too many times and I don't want to revisit that argument.

Her office is empty so I loop around through the kitchen and into the living room. Emma is sprawled out on the couch, laptop sitting on her thighs and her back arched in what looks to be a ridiculously uncomfortable position. Her eyes are glued to her screen as her fingers fly over the keyboard and I use this opportunity to watch her work.

Her long hair is piled on top of her head and she is wearing that *Mario* t-shirt from the other night. I teased her about how she looked, but the truth is, she looks damn sexy. She has a cute crease between her brows as she stops typing, her eyes scanning the screen as she reads.

I wait as she finishes, smirking when she lifts her eyes and yelps at the sight of me.

"Shit! You startled me!" She smiles as I take a seat at her feet. "What brings you by?"

"I wanted to see you. Work away, I'll sit and wait until you're done." She looks torn, but she starts typing again, moaning when I start massaging one of her feet.

We sit like this for a while and it feels so right. I switch to the other foot, making sure I pay just as much attention as I did to the first. Emma shuts her laptop and sets it on the table, leaning her head back and watching me.

"What would you do if you won a million dollars?"

She ponders my question for a bit, but when Chloe bumps her hand with her nose she looks at me. "I would start a rescue for bully breeds. They are so misunderstood and if I had that much money at my disposal I could help the animals and spend time educating people." Guilt floods me as once again she demonstrates what an amazing person she is. We lost days because of my ego and I regret that.

"If you were a tree, what kind of tree would you be?" Emma's voice cuts into my thoughts and I look at her confused.

"Is that a serious question?"

"Yes. Stop looking so serious. We're moving forward." She actually waggles her finger at me. Laughing, I raise my hands in surrender and think about trees.

"I've really never put any thought into it. I don't know what kind of tree I would be, but I know what you would be. You're like a willow tree. They are flexible, bending in the wind and under the weight of snow but it takes a lot to break them. They are deceptive looking in their grace which hides their inner strength. You remind me of a willow tree, except the only one underestimating your strength is you."

Her jaw drops and her eyes search mine as she grasps for something to say. We watch each other in silence, I want her to really think about what I'm saying.

She wrings her hands together, fidgeting as she battles whatever is going on inside. Sitting here, not pulling her into my arms physically hurts, my muscles twitching to move her into me but I fight myself. The moment she has worked through her thoughts is clear, her eyes are vibrant and her face shows a sereneness that has been missing since she fell back into my life.

Shifting on the couch, I wrap my arms around her waist pulling her over so she's sitting on my lap. Emma lays her head on my chest, her breaths matching my heartbeat.

"If I'm a willow tree, you're a spruce tree. Regardless of the season you provide enduring care and shelter to those you love. Even when pushed to the brink, you weather the storm." Her soft voice breaks the quiet and I hold her tighter to me.

Clinging to each other, I lift her chin and gently kiss her lips. She smiles at me and my lips lift in return, the seriousness of the moment passing as we both release the tension still plaguing us from this morning. I have failed to weather the storm once and I will never make that mistake again.

"Most embarrassing moment?" My lips twitch as a blush spreads in her cheeks.

"You're never going to let me live that down, are you?" Her hands press against her face and she scrunches her nose at me.

"Live what down?" My stomach shudders with repressed laughter as she pouts at me.

"Falling into that damn water trough was my most humiliating moment. I think ever!" Emma's head drops as she tries to hide her gaze. I burst into laughter, unable to hold it in any longer. I laugh even harder when she looks up at me, eyes narrowed, and sticks out her tongue.

"What about that time you did a cartwheel and your pants tore? Or what about the time you cut your own hair at it stuck straight out in the front?" Her face scrunches up even more as I list things and she tries to move back to the other side of the couch, but I wrap my arms tightly around her holding her in place. Her playful struggles are arousing me and my hands itch to pin her down again, instead I hold her close until she stills.

"Why? Why remember those moments? Ugh, those were bad, but I was a kid. Now I'm an adult with apparently very little awareness of my surroundings." Emma starts laughing with me. The throaty sound is so sexy it takes my breath away. My laughter dies as I watch her eyes glisten with humor at herself.

All the strings of self-control I had been maintaining snap and I flip her onto her back, laying over her and press my lips to hers. A soft moan hums in her throat as I push into her harder, deepening the kiss and devouring her. There is no stopping this time.

CHAPTER FIFTEEN

Emma

Tangling my hands into Dane's hair, I suck his lower lip into my mouth before biting it gently. The growl that rips from his chest is pure sex and I'm dripping wet. If he pulls away from me this time I will not be held accountable for my actions.

Dane's lips trail hot kisses down my neck to my shoulder, finding that sensitive sweet spot right where the neck and shoulder join. Tilting my head, shivers wrack my body as he thrusts his hips into mine. Dane lifts his head, looking into my eyes I see his pupils are dilated with desire, his chest heaving as he holds himself back.

Pushing him up, I get off the couch and grab his hand. Pulling him through the house and up the stairs, as soon as my bedroom door is closed I'm being lifted and carried across the room, Dane's lips moving against mine fervently. The kiss is hard and passionate, both of us pushing into each other desperately.

He sets me on the ground and we're stripping out of our clothes like two teenagers having sex for the first time and not wanting to get caught. My eyes widen as his erection springs free from his jeans.

"Wow." Dane laughs and I can feel the heat spreading through my cheeks as I realize I said that out loud. His eyes burn as he looks at me, my hands twitch with the need to do something so instead of standing there, I push him onto my bed and straddle him. Dane allows me to take control, watching me hungrily as I trail kisses over his chest and down his stomach.

Lifting my gaze, I hold eye contact as I wrap my lips around his cock, sliding them down rapidly and sucking.

"Holy shit . . ." Dane's hips thrust up and I teasingly pull away from him until they rest on the bed again. Swirling my tongue over his tip; I lick, suck, and nip until he grips my arms and flips me onto my back, his lips meeting my breast. My nipples pucker as he teases them with his tongue, my back arches into him as I fist the sheets in my hands.

I can't believe we're finally doing this. My body is on fire and my head is full of Dane. Everything about this moment feels right. There is a fire in my veins I've never felt before and an affection in each touch that caresses my soul.

The feeling of his thumb pressing onto my clit has me gasping, my body pushing into his as two fingers push inside me, building me up until I'm panting. Whimpering when he pulls away, I watch as he rolls on a condom before settling himself between my legs.

We both groan as he pushes in and my body is pulsating as he begins to move.

"Fuck, you're so tight." Dane's voice is gruff as I clench around him, moving my hips to meet his. Faster and faster, sweat beads down our chests and my eyes are locked with his.

"Harder." My voice is hoarse, my body aching as I near climax and he thrusts harder and faster. My orgasm explodes through me as my entire body tenses, clenching around him in pleasure. Dane's muscles ripple as he moves, his eyes locked on mine as his release rushes through him before he mutters my name and collapses beside me. His lips find mine and he kisses me passionately before he gets up to discard the condom.

Crawling back in bed, he pulls me into his arms and rests his forehead on mine.

"One position down." My jaw drops as he winks at me. Clenching my thighs together, I think of all the other things we have to try and lick my lips. He groans and kisses me hard before laying his head down on the pillow. "I love the way you think, but we have an early morning."

Curling into him, I listen as his breathing deepens, my eyes growing heavy. Feeling his presence and the strength and safety in his arms there is no fear of a nightmare as I finally lose consciousness.

Chloe prances at my feet as I jog around the pen with my horses. My body feels free and relaxed so I pick up speed, a smile spreading as Chloe jumps and barks. She is feeling extra playful today so I end my run, quickly feeding the horses before finding one of Chloe's toys and we play fetch while we wait for Dane to return. Normally Alex is making coffee when I get up in the morning but his door was still closed. Now that my mind isn't preoccupied, I wonder how their evening went.

Dane appears from the barn, grinning as he saunters over to me. His sleeves are rolled up, arms bared making me swoon a little. His eyes twinkle as he wraps an arm around my waist pulling me into him to kiss me. My body turns to mush as the feel of his hard body pressed against mine reminds me of the amazing shower sex we had this morning.

"Two positions down, I wonder if either are your favorite," he whispers in my ear. My knees quiver as moisture pools between my legs and I pull back.

"We'll never know until we try them all." Dane lowers his head and softly kisses me again.

"We have plenty of time to explore them, I'm not letting you go." His voice is low and gravelly as he looks at me unwavering, probing. Holding my breath and body still while he searches until he looks away and takes a deep breath. When he returns his eyes to mine they are burning, calculating how much time we have until breakfast.

"Hey, guys! Ready for breakfast?" Lifting our heads at Alex's voice, Dane forces a smile at him.

"Yes, we are. Let's go." Together we head to breakfast, my brain spinning from the intense moment with Dane and ways to get him and Alex to work through the tension.

Dane

"They're so sweet! It's been too long since I've spent time around foals." Emma's voice is filled with excitement as we ride to the hitching post. She's ties Serenity before climbing the fence, jumping down to the other side with excitement. Her eyes light up as she walks towards the closest of the babies and I lean against the fence to watch her. There is one baby in particular I think she'll love and I'm waiting to see her reaction.

"You can tell how much time you have put into socializing

them!" Emma's voice is soft as she rubs a sorrel filly's nose. Unable to stand back any longer, I swing over the fence and join her, petting a sweet black colt that joins up with me.

"That one is a suck for attention, she is going to be smart and a handful." Emma talks in a low voice to the filly before walking over to the black colt standing next to me. Her hand halts mid-reach when she sees her. Her eyes widen and she looks at me with an even bigger smile.

"You didn't tell me one of the mares threw a palomino."

"I wanted to surprise you, I knew you would love her."

"Her?" Emma walks slowly towards the filly, as though she's scared it's all in her imagination. For as long as I have known Emma she has always had a fondness for horses that are not as common. Buckskins, Grullos, Palominos, and Blue Roans were always her favorites.

The filly prances around her, but stills under her gentle touch. Emma exudes confidence when walking around the horses, but in this moment she is quivering with excitement. The filly sniffs her hair and Emma giggles a sound of pure joy.

"She doesn't have a name yet, want to name her?" Emma nods, completely enraptured with the filly.

"What should your name be, my sweet?" Watching her with the horse fills me with contentment. In this moment everything I have dreamed of is in reach, I just need to get her to where I am.

I have loved Emma since I was eight years old. She had fallen while we were riding and was crying because she twisted her ankle in the landing. In that moment, seeing her hurting and upset I knew I would do anything to make her better. That feeling has only grown over time and the woman she has become surpasses every dream I've ever had.

Smiling at Emma as she continues to stroke the filly's nose, pondering names, I think about all the things I want to do with her.

"I have it! Her name should be Arwen. It stands for noble maiden." Her smile is radiant as she hugs Arwen.

"It's perfect. She is going to be a wonderful addition to your herd." Holding my breath, I wait for her reaction.

The moment my words sink in, Emma flings herself into my arms and I'm instantly aroused as her legs wrap tightly around my waist. Her velvety soft tongue diving into my mouth. Groaning as she pulls my hair, I kiss her harder. Her body moves against mine, rubbing against the bulge in my jeans. Too soon she drops her legs, her body sliding down mine tauntingly. But instead of parting, she steps into my arms, enfolding herself in me.

"She's perfect. Thank you so much." She walks back over to Arwen and kisses her on the nose. Petting her adoringly before glancing at her phone as an alarm sounds. Sighing with regret, she turns away from the babies. "We should head back to the house. I have some writing to do."

"I don't have anything to get done today, can I come hang out? Maybe I can try to get to know Alex, you know now that he's not threatening me." Emma laughs.

"You're more than welcome to come hang out, but I fear you'll be bored."

"No, I won't, I promise."

Watching Alex and Emma work is fascinating. They distract each other and then scold each other for being distracting. Yet it seems to work. I've been watching them for a couple of hours while attempting to get some paperwork done. I'm more successful at watching them.

Alex shuts his laptop and goes to the kitchen. Emma doesn't even look up so I follow him.

"So, Emma tells me you do web design?" He gestures to the coffee and I nod.

"Yes, I designed Emma's if you've ever looked at it. I also help her with her covers and teasers. If you ever need help with a site for the ranch or your training program, please let me know." His offer leaves me speechless and we drink the coffee he has prepared in silence for a bit. Glancing over my shoulder, Emma is still completely engrossed in typing.

"I really appreciate the offer. The website we have is pretty basic and I would like to revamp it. I have been thinking of expanding what we do here and training is a good way to go. So far I only train our own horses before selling them. You know, both Lia and Ryan could probably use help on their websites as well."

"Thanks, if they would like one I have time so send them my way." Silence awkwardly descends and I gulp at my coffee, looking back at Emma.

Emma. Maybe once we discuss her and our relationship it will get less awkward.

"I think we should address the elephant in the room. Thank you for the other night. I had my head up my ass and needed the swift kick to dislodge it. I'm just sorry that is the first impression you had of me." Alex pierces me with a stare, I hold his gaze and stand perfectly still. He evaluates me before setting me free and looks towards Emma.

Following his gaze, I watch her as she remains in her bubble. She tilts her head to the side, fingers pausing on the keyboard while she thinks about something.

"Honestly, if Emma and you are good then we're good. I see the way you look at her, I know you love her." Smiling in relief, we both finally relax.

Then his words sink in. Am I that obvious? Needing time to think about his statement, I search for a new topic.

"How's her book coming?" I've been meaning to ask, but in the past two days we've been a little preoccupied.

"Good, but it's not the conclusion to her series. She's writing something new."

"Oh really? I'll have to ask about it. I've read all her books." Alex looks shocked yet impressed and we share a genuine smile. Conversation begins to flow more smoothly and we find we share a lot in common.

"Dude! Linkin Park's concert was epic!" Alex and I are talking loudly about our favorite concerts when Emma wraps her arms around my waist.

"I think I'm done for today. I'm exhausted and I can't see straight. What are you guys talking about?" Her voice vibrates over my back causing tingles to shoot down my spine. My eyes roll back in my head and Alex laughs at me.

"Your boyfriend got to see Linkin Park in concert!"

Emma releases me so she can gape with Alex. "Seriously? Ugh! I want to see them so badly!" She returns her arms to my waist and starts nuzzling my side.

"All right, on that note . . . I think I'm going to go for a drive and do some exploring. Dane, we should all go to Linger one of these nights. That is a fantastic pub!" He kisses Emma on the side of the head affectionately.

We watch Alex leave the room before I tilt my head down and capture Emma's lips with my own. She wraps her hands around my neck, leaning in before breaking away too soon.

"Dane, I think I need a nap. This book is seriously draining me." She yawns and her eyes do have a glazed quality.

"Alex said you're writing something new. What's it about?" She grabs my hand and starts pulling me upstairs.

"Oh, it's hard to say exactly what kind of story it will be at this point." Emma avoids my gaze as we lay down and I feel like she's hiding something from me, but I ignore it and wrap her into my arms.

"Well, I look forward to reading it." She nods and closes her eyes, starting to doze off.

"Emma?"

"Mmmm."

"I love you." I know she's awake because her body stills. When she pretends to sleep I let it slide, disappointment filling me despite knowing she's not ready to repeat the sentiment yet. One day she will realize she loves me too and I will hear those words from her lips.

CHAPTER SIXTEEN

Emma

"I had the best visit with Arwen today." Lia pops a chip into her mouth, grinning as I gush about my new filly. It's been a few days since Dane gave her to me and I've gone to see her every day.

"I'm glad. I'll have to come with you to see her soon. Hey! We should set up a weekly riding date! I need girl time and I feel like your time is being hogged, not that I'm not thrilled about you and Dane." She winks at me.

"That's a great idea. We can work it into your schedule." We're looking at Lia's schedule trying to pick the best time when Alex walks into the room and bursts into laughter at our spread.

"Why hello, ladies. I forgot it's girl's night. I'm heading to Linger with Dane, Ryan, and Jesse. They were nice enough to let me tag along. Want me to crash in my truck?" He winks at us both and if I'm not imagining things, Lia blushes. I've noticed the two of them making eyes at each other, but to my knowledge nothing has happened. Watching them now though, I wonder.

"Don't be ridiculous. Lia will sleep with me."

"Okay! Have fun, don't get sick on all that junk food." He grins widely at us before leaving.

"So, Lia, you and Alex . . . Has something happened there?" Her blush deepens, but she shakes her head.

"He flirts, I flirt back. It's nothing. Things are going well with Dane, I take it?"

Letting the subject change slide, I look down and take a deep breath. "He told me he loves me."

"What?" Lia squeals so loudly Chloe jumps up to check on her. Laughing, Lia pushes her down gesturing wildly at me to continue.

"Lia, I pretended to sleep, but I think he knows I was awake. I feel so guilty over it, but saying it back is a huge step. How do I know I'm ready?" I feel deflated as I unload the thoughts that have been taking up too much brain space. I've never been such a coward before, I want the old me back not this weak and scared new version.

"Hun, I think you already know. Dane will be patient, he truly loves you."

Taking a deep breath, I sit up straighter and resolve to be stronger. "I've booked an appointment with a counselor this coming Wednesday. I need to start addressing my grief and anxiety more seriously. I haven't told anyone but you."

"Why not?"

"I will, I just need to get through the first month or so first, make sure I like the counselor and whatnot. I've been back home for over a month now and, while things are better, I've realized I need help. I don't want to be this way anymore. I know that the way I'm being affected by the car accident and Grandpa's heart attack isn't normal. The fear of losing more people to the point of wanting to shut myself down from getting too close, that's not healthy. I need help."

Lia wraps an arm around me resting her head on my shoulder. "I'm proud of you, Em, I know it's not easy to admit you need help. You will get there because you truly want to." Lia rubs her hands together gleefully. "Okay! It was my night to plan the fun. Instead of watching movies, I thought we could play some good old *Mario* Kart!" Lia is bouncing as she waits for my reaction, if this was a cartoon my eyes would be rolling. She's making me dizzy.

"Yes! That sounds like so much fun! Now please stop bouncing before you give me motion sickness." Lia jumps up and quickly sets up her N64, passing me a controller.

"Nooo!" Lia screams at the TV as I blow up her last balloon. We're both sitting on the floor, directly in front of the TV, hunched over and staring at the screen.

"Boom! You suck . . ." I can't help the gloating tone to my voice.

Lia sets her controller down and turns to me, a glint in her eyes. "That's it. *Smash Bros* time."

"No! You know I've never been good at that game." Throwing myself on the ground as she switches games, I reach for my phone when it beeps with a text.

"No phones!" Lia tries to grab it from me.

"It's from Dane. C'mon. Just one?" She rolls her eyes and turns back to the TV.

> Dane: What is your favorite thing about yourself?

His question makes me pause. It's not something I think about much, but in the spirit of trying to work on my issues I take his question seriously.

> Me: This question is hard, but I love how I know myself, what I want and I go for it. At least that's how I used to be and I will be again.

Setting my phone down, I take the controller from Lia and we start playing again. My body feels rigid and I focus on relaxing. Fingers flying over the buttons on the controller, Lia yelling at her character and my thoughts drowning in my response, I will be that girl again . . . One day.

~

Dane

"Put your damn phone away!" Ryan yells at me over the noise of Linger. He and Alex just finished a game of pool and bought us a round of beer. Alex offered to be our designated driver so after his first two, he's been drinking water.

Tucking my phone back in my pocket, I feel it vibrate with Emma's response and resist the urge to check it. Jesse has finished grilling Alex and nodded his approval. Jesse's been leery of new people for as long as I've known him, but Alex took his interrogation in good stride. Thankfully now that we've gotten to know each other, I can admit that the guy is pretty cool.

"Dane, I hate to be the bearer of bad news, but Yvette just walked in the door and is making eyes at you." Ryan jerks his chin in her direction. Turning my head slightly, I see her at the bar staring at me.

"I just hope she stays over there." Groaning, I angle my body away from her.

"Who is that?" Alex looks between Yvette and me curiously.

"I went on three dates with her and she has been persistent in her advances despite being told I'm not interested. She has a streak of crazy that I didn't know about and I'm telling you now, keep your distance." I play with the label on my beer bottle.

"Jesse, are you excited to start at the ranch?" Ryan changes the subject with a knowing look in my direction and I'm glad we're moving past that crazy ass woman. My gut clenches when I see her, there is something about her that makes me uneasy.

I tune back into the conversation and hear the last half of what Jesse is saying. ". . . great to be outdoors. Actually, Dane, I can start whenever. I finished up my project and I'm free as a bird now!"

"Fantastic man. I can already tell you're enjoying being free of that place." He's more relaxed and hasn't stopped smiling all evening. He seems more at peace and it feels great knowing I could help my friend out.

"Oh yeah. The people were fine and the job was fine, but you know at some point you get tired of living just being fine. It was the first step, the next is going to be more challenging."

"What's next?" I'm curious at the cautious tone in Jesse's voice. He sits tall as he ponders whether or not to tell us, his eyes reserved. Grabbing his beer, he takes a deep drink before crossing his arms.

"I need to come out to my parents."

Crickets.

His words sink in and we sit in silence. Jesse grabs his beer again, gulping it down while we sit in shock. No one moves. Alex sits awkwardly, new to this group and he just smiles at Jesse encouragingly. I don't care that my best friend is gay, but I'm surprised I never put it together.

I grip Jesse's shoulder and smile at him. "Good for you. If you need anything you know we've got your back." Jesse breathes a sigh of relief and nods, a brilliant smile on his face.

We all lean back in the booth, relaxing and chatting.

"I want to get some wings. You guys in?" They all nod so I head to the bar to order.

"I'll come. That chick looks like she's ready to tie you up and drag you outta here." Alex walks over with me and we order. "What's her deal anyways?"

"I'm not really sure. She wasn't bad until the third date and it was little things she would say, nothing specific. But the continuous texts and phone calls, it's been months, I finally blocked her number. I quit going on dates as soon as I found out Em was moving back."

Alex looks over my shoulder and grimaces. A hand wraps around my biceps and I'm assaulted with perfume.

"Hi, Dane." Yvette's voice is sugary sweet, fake.

Turning towards her, I gently pull my arm from her grasp and back up so I'm standing next to Alex. His look of disdain would be comical, but my body is too busy fighting its flight response. "Hi."

Examining her now, I don't know what I ever saw in her. Her eyes are cynical and calculating, her smile plastered and fake. These make her otherwise pretty features disappear because they are swallowed into the ugliness inside. Having Emma back in my life has made this so much clearer. Her inner beauty, her kindness just makes how stunning she is on the outside shine so much more.

"Saw you looking my way, have you changed your mind about going out again? We could go dance." She smiles at me, running a finger down my chest.

My feet move on their own, stepping away from her. "No thanks. Like I said, not interested." I'm trying to be polite, but my voice is firm. Instead of leaving like a normal woman who has been shot down several times would, she steps closer.

"C'mon. Just one dance."

"I've said this before and I will say it again. For the last time. No. I'm not interested and I doubt my girlfriend would look at it as just one dance." My voice is like razor blades and her eyes widen in shock as she steps back at the force of my words. Alex shakes his head at her before stepping between us and turning his back to her.

Yvette leaves in a huff, a haze of perfume left in her wake. "Holy shit that woman is persistent, and seriously, her perfume should be classified as a noxious gas!" We move down the bar trying to escape the cloud of gag-inducing scent, my body buzzing.

"Hopefully she finally gets the hint. Although, blocking her number didn't seem to help."

Two plates of chicken wings are set down before us and my mouth starts watering.

"Those smell so good. Thanks, Dylan." We smile at the bartender and carry the plates back to our table, Jesse and Ryan digging in before they are even set on the table.

"Did you guys shower in perfume while you were over there?" Jesse starts coughing as he catches a whiff of whatever Yvette doused herself in, waving his hands in front of his nose.

"I wish. Yvette decided to pay us a visit." I fill them in and they cheer when I tell them I think she's finally going to back off.

Grinning at my buddies as they eat, I slide my phone out of my pocket and read Emma's reply. I may be reading too much into it, but her text makes me smile. There is the fighter I know is in there. Her text has conviction to it and I may be assuming this but I feel like part of it is referring to our relationship.

CHAPTER SEVENTEEN

Emma

I wake up to the sound of my bedroom door opening and force my eyes open. Lia is slipping in my room, gently closing it behind her.

"Lia?" She jumps at the sound of my voice and I laugh groggily. "What are you doing?"

"I went downstairs to let Chloe out and get some water." Sitting up, I take in her appearance. She looks a little disheveled and flushed.

"Are you okay? You look a little flushed. Are you sick?" Lia sits next to me and I place my hand on her forehead. "Your temp is okay."

"Stop being a worry wart. I'm fine. Chloe didn't want to come in, is that okay?"

"Yeah, she's fine. She won't go anywhere." Crawling out of bed, I grab some clothes and head into the bathroom.

Lia is changed when I come out. "I missed our sleepovers.

Even when we're old and gray we need to make sure we still have sleepovers."

"Of course. We're going to sit in our rockers on the porch, cracking dirty jokes." She laughs as I scrunch my face up and start dirty talking in my best imitation of an old woman's voice.

"Seriously, that voice is creepy." She shudders as we leave my room, running into Alex in the hall.

"What voice?" Alex's hair is damp, the fresh scent of his shampoo filling the air around us.

"My old lady impersonation. You smell nice. Who are you trying to impress?" Wrapping an arm around him I give him a half hug.

"Oh yeah, that is creepy. And I figured I was waking up to two beautiful women, the least I can do is be decently clean." He smiles at us and I jab him with my elbow. Flirt. He's always been a smooth talker, too bad he can't seem to find the right girl.

"Well, I'm going to go start breakfast." Lia opens the door, pausing when Alex rests his hand on her shoulder, a pink hue filling her cheeks. Sucking in my bottom lip to keep from smirking, I watch their interaction with interest.

"Don't rush out of here. I thought I would come help you. Just let me grab something from the kitchen." My eyes flick between them suspiciously, as his hand lingers on her shoulder, twirling some of her hair between his fingers. Alex smiles at me as he walks away, but Lia avoids my gaze.

She has a secret.

"What's going on with you two?" I grin at her when she lifts her head, eyes wide.

"Nothing! How can anything be going on? We barely know each other." Her voice is slightly breathless and I chuckle at her attempt at nonchalance.

"Uh huh. Okay. Stay in denial, but I know you as well as you know me." Alex comes back and I grin as we walk out of the house together. "I shouldn't be too long."

Dane is waiting for me as I finish up with my horses. I spent some extra time brushing them since I've been paying so much attention to Arwen lately.

"Good morning, beautiful." He kisses me before linking his fingers with mine. His rough hand is warm and tingles shoot up my arm from where his thumb gently strokes circles on the inside of my wrist. Heart beating faster than normal, I enjoy the happiness that fills me just being in his presence.

"Morning." He chuckles as I groan out the word, eyes rolling into the back of my head as his thumb continues to tease the sensitive spot on my wrist. He knows exactly what he is doing to me and he is reveling in it.

We get to the door and I pull my hand from Dane's, stopping on their porch. The heat from our contact dissipating as a strange urge fills me.

"What's wrong?"

"Go on in, I just need a moment." He looks at me in concern, I grab his hand and squeeze. "I'm fine. I'll be right in."

Dane heads into the house and I sit on the bench. Maybe it's finally feeling some happiness again, maybe it's that I've finally accepted my need for help, but my heart burns with a need I've been resisting.

"Mom . . . Dad . . . Grandpa . . . I don't know if you're listening, I like to think that you are. I miss you so much and I wish I could talk to you every day. I'm sorry that it's taken me so long to talk to you, to start pulling myself back together. Being home has helped and I think I'm finally starting to accept the way things are. I love you and I feel good about starting counselling. I also wanted to tell you that Dane makes me so happy,

I'm falling for him which is scary as hell. I really wish you were here."

Standing up, I wipe a tear off my cheek. I feel at peace finally having acknowledged them in the only way I can. In just over a month and a half, August 20th, it will be the one year anniversary of my parents' death and a month after that is the one year anniversary of Grandpa passing away. Walking into the kitchen, I smile as I take in my new family, my new reality. I can do this.

I climb into my truck and rest my forehead on the steering wheel. My second counselling session just finished and somehow I started talking about my guilt over my parents' accident. My eyes feel raw from crying and I know they are puffy and red. I need a nap.

At least my nerves weren't as bad on the way to therapy as they were last week. I had to pull over three times to ward off anxiety attacks on the way there alone.

Heart pounding, head spinning and lungs collapsing, I pull over to the side of the road. How can I talk openly and honestly to a stranger about my weakness? How can I admit that I'm at fault for my parents dying? Or that I didn't make more of an effort to see Grandpa even though he was getting older? Tears fall as I choke on the air I'm trying to inhale. For the longest time I buried the guilt, was in denial. But now it's in the forefront of my mind.

My heart hurts so damn bad. They were my world. The loss of them. The hole that will never be filled. It burns, the pain and guilt. The blackness that fills my mind, always present . . . Taunting.

Shaking off the memory of last week, I bring myself back into the present.

Pulling in a deep breath, I sit up and start my truck.

The drive disappears in a blur as my thoughts swirl around my therapy session with Dr. Hughes. She has strongly recommended I talk to my friends about my feelings of guilt, that it will help release it by admitting to it. She asked me to talk to at least one of my friends this week. I committed to telling Alex, ease into it.

The relief at opening up to her is still a shock and her non-judgmental attitude makes it easy to talk to her. Yet it still terrifies me to think about how others may react when I open up to them about where Mom and Dad were going.

Dr. Hughes was emphatic that the accident was not my fault, it was a tragic accident, but I wonder how others will see it.

Chloe runs towards the truck as I park and sits patiently while I pull my bag out before crouching down and scratching her head. This dog always knows when I need her.

"Dane came by looking for you. He seemed confused that no one knew where you went. Where were you?" Alex leans against the truck, crossing his legs. His voice is chastising as he continues. "It's the second week in a row that you've disappeared without telling anyone where you've gone. That's not cool, Em. Dane was worried. I was worried." The look of disappointment on Alex's face upsets me. I hate disappointing him and worrying him, but I'm pissed off that I can't leave my house for two hours without being hounded.

"I'm sorry I worried you, but last time I checked I'm allowed to leave the house for two fucking hours without checking in. I love that you care enough to worry, but seriously? Two hours?" The stress from my session and my irritation at Alex flows out of me as my voice gets louder and louder. Alex's face breaks out in a smile and I scowl at him. I'm downright pissed that first he bitches at me and then laughs at me. "What is so funny?"

"It's been close to a year since I've seen this much spunk from you." He walks over and wraps his arms around me. "You're right, I'm sorry. It's just hard not to worry after the past ten and a half months. I am happy to see you get pissed off though, you haven't had the energy to react so strongly in a long time. Now, seriously, where were you? I'm asking because I love you and because I'm interested in what's going on in your life."

We start walking to the house, my fingers fidgeting with my bag strap. Breathing becomes a struggle as my nerves fight to let coward in me take over. Fighting back, I force the breath and find some strength. Hands sweating with the strain of talking about this, even to Alex, I finally whisper the words, "I started seeing a therapist to address my grief and anxiety."

Alex halts in the doorway, a stunned look on his face. Slamming the door, he picks me up and swings me around. "I'm so proud of you! How's it going?"

His exuberance is slightly overwhelming as I continue to struggle inside. I hate the fast fluttering of my heart and the fire in my lungs. Anger fills me at what I've become and I mentally fight back. Despite the fear filling me, the weakness that's always ready at my core, I manage to process his question.

"Hard, but honestly, it's helping. Last week was my first session and I told her what happened. This week was a surprise to me. We discussed my nightmares, I told her I had one last week after our session, but that it wasn't as bad as they have been previously. Then out of nowhere I told her something no one knows." Taking a deep breath, I sit at the counter as Alex pours me a glass of water. "I told her that my parents died because of me. If my car wouldn't have broken down they wouldn't have been driving." Staring down at the counter, I watch Alex from my peripheral vision and force myself to breathe.

Breathe in. Hold for ten. Breathe out.

Alex stares at me until water overflows from the glass. Grabbing a towel, he wipes the water while vigorously shaking his head. He pauses, looks at me and then passes me my water in silence.

Breathe in. Hold for ten. Breathe out.

Dr. Hughes suggested this technique and surprisingly, or maybe not all that surprising, it helps.

"I know what you're thinking. It's not my fault. This is why I'm telling you, Dr. Hughes felt that sharing my thoughts will help."

"I know nothing I say can change your mind, but I'm still going to say it. You are not the reason that your parents died. The truck driver was under the influence of alcohol. All you did was what anyone would, called and asked for help." Alex's voice is strong, sure, and emphatic. Relief floods me that he reacted in this manner, guilt nags at me for doubting him, anger and fear fade as I continue to breathe. This is exhausting.

"You're right. I absolutely know that you're right, but those feelings don't just go away. It's something I need to work through. Now I need to go have a nap. Therapy is emotionally tiring and I need to sleep it off." I gulp down the rest of my water, putting my glass into the dishwasher.

"When are you going to talk to Dane? If you love him, he should be included in this."

"Wait . . . Love?" Staring at him, frozen in place. I'm not ready to be in love, I'm still so broken, so weak.

"Yes, love. He deserves to know." Alex gently pushes me out of the kitchen. "Now go nap."

Walking up the stairs in a haze, my mind is stuck on repeat.

Breathe in. Hold for ten. Breathe out.

Laying down, Chloe at the foot of my bed, I close my eyes and as I fall asleep, I'm thinking about Dane. Do I love him?

When I think about him I feel happy. My heart jumps enthusiastically even just remembering things he's said or done.

Holy shit.

I love him.

When did that happen?

I need to tell him.

~

Dane

Walking into Emma and Alex's kitchen, disappointment and worry fills me when I see Alex on the couch in the living room working at his laptop without Emma. Normally at this time in the afternoon she and Alex are crowded together on her couch working. She's home, her truck is back, but I still haven't seen her. I'm trying to be patient, but she's been acting weird over the past week and a half. Disappearing twice now, no one knowing where she went.

"Where's Emma?" Alex looks up from his laptop, glasses crooked on his face. I can't help but laugh, gesturing with my hands until he fixes them with a shrug.

"Upstairs napping. I told her we were worried and she went off on me that she's a grown woman. Honestly once the shock wore off, it was nice to see some of her old self show through." Alex makes room for me on the couch and I join him.

"Ugh, she's right. I feel like a tool." Leaning back on the

couch, I sigh as I relax for the first time today. "How's the new website coming along?"

"I think it looks fantastic, but I'm biased. Want to see?" Nodding, I lean in as he shows me the updates he's done to the ranch's web page. It's laid out clearly, highlighting the new training program I'm starting now that Jesse has lightened my regular workload.

"Great work! It's nice and clear, not overloaded like it was. I like how you added in links to Ryan and Lia's sites."

"Thanks man! I thought since you all work in conjunction with each other it was appropriate. Is the banner okay?"

He designed a logo for the ranch and the simplicity while hitting all the points of what we offer is perfect.

"Wow! It's better than I could have imagined." Alex smiles with pride and hands me his computer so I can explore the pages. Seeing the pictures in the gallery of the foals reminds me that we need to move them. "Hey, I need to start moving the foals to their own pen. Would you like to help? Since you've been riding and working with the horses, you have a natural talent for it by the way, I thought you might like to experience other aspects of ranch life."

Alex and I have become good friends and I've been helping Emma give him lessons. Now that he's discovered the joy of riding and spending time with the horses he is eager to learn.

"Absolutely. Any way I can help around here, I'm game. I'm going to finish up making these changes for your final approval." Alex takes the computer back from me and starts tapping away, so I head upstairs to check on Emma.

Her door is slightly ajar and I peer inside. Emma lies on her side, curled in a ball; silent tears streaking down her face. Her eyes are moving rapidly under her lids. A fierce need to protect her and stop the pain fills me. She owns my heart and all it wants is to repair hers.

Entering her room, I shut the door behind me before gently crawling over her. I lie down and curl up behind her, tucking her trembling body into me tightly and wrapping my arm securely around her. This nightmare is nothing like the previous one I saw. What could make this one so drastically different?

"Emma. Wake up." Kissing her softly by her ear, I speak soothingly until her eyes open and she turns into my arms, burying her face into my shoulder crying softly. Swallowing the lump that forms in my throat, I hold her as tightly as I can without hurting her. We lay in silence, nothing I say will make the pain go away.

I want to make the pain go away. Frustration at being unable to do anything threatens to consume me, but I focus on the beautiful woman in my arms.

Her cries subsiding, she pulls back and looks at me with a sad smile. "You know how they say the loss of someone gets easier with time? Whoever said that lied."

"It's not easier; you just learn to live again. You learn how to look at times with a smile because you're simply happy that you had those times at all, not because it's easier. When someone is ripped from your life so drastically you think about all the things you wish you could have said. The last things you wish you could have done. Most of all, you wish you could have held them one more time and told them you love them one last time."

"I don't want them to fade. I don't want to push their memory away anymore because I've realized that hurts almost more than losing them. It hurts so much knowing there is no last time, but I also know it will hurt even more if I look back on how I've survived without them in shame. The three of them, they taught me to be strong. They taught me that when I set my mind to something, I can achieve it. I'm no longer going to float through life without them as a shadow of the person I once was because when I'm up there with them; I want them to smile at me with pride, not look at me with sadness at the life I chose to live."

Hugging Emma closer, my heart aches for her. In the month and a half she's been back, this is the most she has said to me about the accident and her feelings. We still haven't discussed her panic attack in the car, instead when we drive any distance we all pile into her truck and she drives, none of us wanting to push her when she isn't ready.

Pulling in deep breaths, emotions flooding me as her words replay in my head, my mind is filled with images of her time back at home. How had I underestimated just how much she was holding in? She has started to come out from under her veil of guardedness over the past couple of weeks and it has opened my eyes to how much I still need to learn, silly questions game aside, I need to go deeper. She still holds so much in and my need to know is constantly simmering underneath the surface, I'm trying not to push her, but at some point it's going to boil over.

"You're right that they would want you to be happy. To live your life to the fullest and to remember them with a smile on your lips, not tears in your eyes. But I think they would understand how difficult this has been for you. No one expects you to just get over it immediately; I think we worry because you hold everything so close to you. I know you've only been back for a short time, but it has made a difference. Whenever you want to talk, I'm always here for you. I love you and will do whatever I can to help you through this."

Holding her gaze, I watch as emotions flicker through her eyes. I don't think I'm imagining the love I see there, yet she doesn't utter the words back. Instead she leans forward, kisses me gently and whispers something so softly I can't hear it.

Pushing away the disappointment, I smile brightly at her and pull her face back to mine; kissing her with everything I'm feeling. As she returns the kiss passionately, I hope she is using this kiss to tell me what she can't say quite yet.

Laying together in bed, kissing and talking, the sad mood from her dream slowly disintegrates. Contentment fills me as we go back and forth asking questions before I find I can't keep my hands off her any longer.

Leaning on my elbow, I comb my fingers through her hair before leaning down and kissing her jaw teasingly.

Emma puts her hand on my shoulder, pushing gently and I let her move me onto my back. Groaning as she straddles me, heat burning in her eyes, she undresses without her eyes leaving mine before helping me pull my clothes off. I reach to grab a condom from her drawer but she stops me.

"I'm on the pill. I haven't ever . . . With you, I want to feel everything."

Emma slowly lowers herself onto me, her tight walls gripping me. Moaning at the sensation of being bare to each other, this experience is unlike any other. Emma feels perfect, dripping in her desire for me and it's all I can do to allow her to control the movements. Her body picks up speed as she leans down and kisses me passionately.

Sweat beads on my forehead as I grab her hips and push into her harder, urged on by her frantic moans and hands gripping my shoulders like vices.

Sitting up, Emma grabs my hips and moves faster, groaning out my name as she climaxes. The intensity of feeling her release, her body surrounding mine as we experience an intimacy neither of us has before, is almost overwhelming and I need to take control. Flipping her onto her back, I thrust my hips into hers coming hard and fast.

Emma's eyes are filled with passion and the love she

cannot express as I lean down and kiss her before sliding out and lying next to her.

Grabbing her hands into mine, I pull her out of bed with me before wrapping my arms around her. Bending my head down, I kiss her gently, enjoying the way her soft skin feels against mine.

"As much as I would love to spend the rest of the day in bed with you, Lia will have dinner on the table soon and you know she won't hesitate to come storming in here. Risk of emotional scarring and all." Emma laughs and we get dressed quickly.

"We always have after dinner." Emma winks at me suggestively before giggling and sashaying out of the room.

Looking at the ceiling, I think of unsexy things before chasing after her.

CHAPTER EIGHTEEN

Emma

Sitting on the brown leather chair in Dr. Hughes' room, I cross my legs and lean back. Her office is filled with colorful paintings; similar in style to the ones Lia does on occasion. She calls it mixed media. I don't really know what that means, but when I look at these each week I notice something new in the colors and textures.

When I first started seeing Dr. Hughes, her office was a complete surprise. I expected a stuffy white room with a couch that I would lay on and her at my head asking questions and taking notes. Instead the room is a soft yellow, with a huge window, and potted plants in the corners and hanging from the ceiling. There are two leather chairs and a loveseat with a coffee table centered between them. It's cozy and has a natural feel. The artwork adds brightness and despite being here to discuss my weaknesses, I can't help but feel comfortable.

Dr. Hughes smiles at me as she enters the room and sits in the chair next to mine.

"How are you today, Emma?" Dr. Hughes is in her thirties, her voice smooth and gentle. Something about her draws information out of me and I'm grateful we clicked so well.

"I'm doing well. Better than I expected to be."

"Last week was very heavy for the second session, were you able to talk to any of your friends about the guilt you feel over your parents' car accident?"

"Well, I got home and Alex was pestering me where I was so it kind of exploded out that I started seeing a therapist. I did open up about the guilt I feel and he was very supportive. As difficult as it was to tell him, I do feel better. My nightmares have shifted, they aren't as bad and I'm starting to be able to talk to my parents. That sounds a little crazy, doesn't it?"

"Not at all. Quite often the way we maintain a connection to those no longer in our life is to talk to them, kind of like a prayer." Her words make sense and I relax more into my chair. "I'm glad that you talked to Alex. Tell me how the dream after our session played out."

The rest of the hour passes quickly and as I drive home, I prepare to tell Dane everything. My guilt. What happens in my dreams. And most importantly, that I love him. Dr. Hughes suggested once I started opening up and talking about everything I'm struggling with that my anxiety around being in the backseat of the car will begin to improve. I'm skeptical about that, but so far she has been right with everything else.

I quickly give my horses some love before heading into the house, finding Alex in his usual spot on the couch.

"How was counseling?" He looks up, and smiles as he takes me in. "Must have been good, you don't look ready to pass out like last time."

"It was good. I know it's still early in the process, but I feel a huge difference. I'm going to talk to Dane later, confide in him like I know he's waiting for. I'm ready. He's out with Jesse 'til later so I figured I would get some work done."

Alex makes room for me on the couch and I quickly load my document, words turning around in my head eager to be released. This book is nearing completion and I have decided to publish it. Knowing I'm going to open the gate and let Dane in has given me the courage to share it. It's personal, it's emotional, and I know it's some of the best writing I've ever done.

Alex's phone dings with a text. His face lights up with a grin as he reads it and he hurriedly sets his laptop aside.

He notices me watching him curiously and shifts as he stands there, eager to bolt out the door. Instead of saying anything, he kisses me on the forehead and tries to casually saunter away. If I didn't know better, I would think he's going to get laid. Realization strikes and laughter erupts. Oh, this is priceless. He and Lia have both been acting weird around each other and I think I just figured out why.

Looking back at my screen, I shift trying to get comfortable, but it's no use. I need my sweats and t-shirt. Setting my laptop on the island in the kitchen, I race upstairs with Chloe at my heels to change.

Chloe goes racing out the door as I am pulling my jeans off, tail wagging. Crazy dog.

Heading down the stairs, finally in my comfy writing clothes, I smile as I think about seeing Dane later. Maybe we can go for a walk through the trails, sit at the tire swing and I can tell him what's going on.

Rounding the corner into the kitchen, I halt as I see the man occupying my thoughts. The smile is wiped from my face and uncontrollable panic and anger fills me as I watch him read my laptop screen.

The shock dissipates and I storm over, slamming my laptop shut and glare at him.

"What the fuck do you think you're doing?" My body vibrates from anger and fear. I don't want him to read into my writing before I've had a chance to talk to him. The invasion of my privacy rocks me to my core and his expression of surprise barely registers. "Well? How dare you impede on my privacy by reading that?"

"Emma, calm down. It was open and caught my eye. I only . . ." He places his hands on my shoulders trying to placate me, but I pull away. Tears of anger burn behind my eyes and I turn away from him to compose myself. What if he saw through my writing? I was wrong, I'm not ready to tell him and expose my vulnerability. The risk is too great.

"So, you thought that because it was open that it was a free for all? I wasn't aware that was how things worked." My voice is raised to such a high pitch that it hurts even my ears. Chloe stands next to me whimpering and I force myself to lower my voice. "I am so fucking angry right now I'm having a hard time looking at you."

Dane jolts back and grits his teeth, the muscles in his jaw flexing as he stares at me. Hurt. Anger. Fear. Confusion. All those emotions flicker in his eyes and in the back of my head I'm screaming at myself for being unreasonable, but I'm letting my weakness prevail.

Fight it.

Give in.

So weak.

Breathe in. Hold for ten. Breathe out.

"Emma . . ." Dane walks slowly towards me, palms forward, eyes pleading. "Please, I didn't think about it, I shouldn't have looked." His tone is consoling, face panicked and regretful.

I'm weak.

Be strong.

Breathe in. Hold for ten. Breathe out.

"No. You shouldn't have. I just . . . How can I trust . . ." Dane's hands resting on my shoulders cuts off the thought, and I jerk my head back to look into his eyes. His eyes which are full of compassion and love, burning with his need for me to calm down, are my undoing. The tears I've been holding back fall and my shoulders slump as the calm that always comes when Dane touches me starts battling the fear and anger. Closing my eyes, I mentally struggle against the darkness. I'm strong, I can do this. No, I can't . . .

Dane lifts my chin and waits until I open my eyes before looking at me intently, almost like he can see everything going on inside. "Emma, I look into your eyes and I see the demons that haunt you. There is nothing I want more than to replace those demons with myself. I don't ever want to be the cause for that look in your eyes again. Once was enough. I want to be the reason they shine. I want to be the reason you glow and not shake with all these pent-up emotions. I'm all about us, but you need to let me in."

He holds my gaze, I'm captive to it. His green eyes are soft, pleading with me. From deep in my belly I let out the breath I've been holding, and soak up his words mentally feeling them wrap around me. Searching deep within I find the determination I need, wrap his words around it and push away the darkness.

Hands shaking, I lift them to grip his forearms and brace myself in his strength.

With him, I am strong.

He lets out a sigh of relief when I don't throw his hands off my shoulders, still remaining silent while he waits for me to speak. My throat is so dry when I try to talk it comes out as a croak so I let go of his arms and grab a glass of water before sitting on the couch. Dane sits next to me, thigh touching mine and folds my hand into his. Still silent.

"I'm so sorry, Dane. That was completely unreasonable, I just panicked. It's not a good enough excuse, but it's the only one I have. You didn't deserve for me to go off on you like that." Taking a deep breath, I use his strength and finally tell him what I've been doing the past few Wednesdays. "The reason I've been disappearing for two hours a week is because I've started to see a counselor. I know the way that I have dealt with these past eleven months has not been normal and I needed help. I've only gone three times, but I feel a difference. To some it may sound crazy, but I think I was finally ready."

I pause and gauge his reaction before continuing. His face is empathetic and non-judgmental giving me the courage to talk about this. "The night my parents got hit by that truck, I was stranded because my car had broken down again. My parents were coming to get me and it was while they were on their way to me that they got hit. I've blamed myself all this time for their accident and the guilt has been smothering. I still blame myself. It took a long time to voice that guilt, mostly it has lived in my subconscious."

"It's not . . ." Dane's voice is strong and sure, but I cut him off. The need to get this out courses through my veins, like a poison I need to release.

"I know. In my heart, I know that. It's funny though, isn't it? How hard it is sometimes to get your head and your heart to agree and my thoughts can be a dark place. Dr. Hughes is helping me work through that and my dreams have started shifting. They aren't as bad as they were before. They feel brighter, more hopeful, and I think that's because I feel more optimistic."

Closing my eyes, I think through the next words I need to

say. Opening up about the accident and how I feel about it hasn't been as tough as I always thought it would be. Expressing my feelings for Dane is more challenging. He's said he loves me and I see it in the way he looks at me, feel it in the way he touches me. Yet telling him the feelings are reciprocated, it's scary for me. No one has ever made me feel the way he has and the vulnerability of giving him all of me has my heart pounding.

"Emma, you are a remarkable woman and I love every thought, every part of you." He pulls me into his arms, thinking I have shared all that I need to and I allow myself to relax into him for a moment before sitting up and facing him straight on. He tilts his head, eyes questioning and in this moment, I feel the strength I need fill me.

"Dane, ever since you pulled me out of that water trough things have gotten easier. In the car you calmed my panic attack and my nightmares have reduced so much, I'm not scared to sleep anymore. Being here has helped, but most of it is you. Maybe it's our history, but I think it has more to do with how you make me feel. You make me want to live, you make me smile, and you make my pain not feel so heavy." As the words spill from my mouth, I don't even know if they make sense, but they come out stronger, surer. Staring at him, I see happiness and I finally utter the three words hidden in the darkness for too long. "I love you."

Weightless. That is the only way to describe what uttering those three words has made me feel. Completely free for just a moment.

The smile that spreads across his face is so radiant. I feel the rest of the darkness lift and hug him tightly. This man brings light back to my life, this man makes me want to work out my issues and this man is helping make me feel whole again.

Dane

Jesse leads Raven over to where I sit on Charger, tightens the saddle and pulls himself up. He follows my eyes as I watch Emma and Alex get their horses ready. "Dude, you're so smitten. You can't even look away."

"Smitten is for teenagers. I love her and yesterday she told me she loves me too." Grinning widely, I reluctantly look away from her and face my best friend. "Have you talked to your parents yet?" Pursing his lips, he fiddles with his mare's mane and shakes his head. "Why not?"

"Because I'm a fucking chicken. My mom will be fine, but you know how my dad is."

"You need to tell them. Do it this weekend. If you need to go out after and unwind, we can all go to Linger. Who knows, maybe you will meet someone once the weight of keeping it a secret is off your shoulders."

"But..."

"If your dad can't love you for who you are, then fuck him. Don't get me wrong, I adore Alan, but you are his son and he should support you in being happy and true to yourself."

"All right, all right. I will tell him tomorrow, you bossy asshole. But we're going out afterwards, I know I'm going to need a drink." Smiling at him when he concedes, I hide the fear I share with him. His father is a very traditional conservative and this has the potential to put a huge wedge in their relationship.

Alex rides up on Chandler and fist bumps Jesse. While they chat, I move around them and lean over to kiss Emma. Despite spending the night with her, the short time I went to quickly do chores before breakfast felt like torture. It is days like today I wish I could stay in all day, locked away with the woman I love without thinking of anything else.

"We're meeting Ryan and Lia there, they're coming from the clinic." Emma and I ride side by side as we go to separate the foals from their moms. They are old enough to be weaned and Jesse finished checking their new pen to ensure it's safe for them.

"How many foals are we moving?" This is Alex's first time coming to work with the horses and despite the progress he has made, nervousness is apparent in his voice.

"We have twelve foals. I have been handling them since day one and they all lead very well." Lia and Ryan are waiting for us as we walk up. Tossing them the halters, I tie Charger to the hitching post. "The pen they are moving into is the smaller one that is attached, the babies can't feed through the wire but it won't be too much of a separation."

It doesn't take long to move the foals. Jesse, Lia, and Ryan all leave to go back to work, leaving Emma, Alex, and me to ensure they settle in okay.

"Arwen, you're such a pretty girl! I can't wait to bring you home," Emma coos at her horse while Alex and I watch.

"I hear she told you she loves you." Alex smiles at me knowingly when I grin. "I don't need to do the big brother warning do I?"

"I think it's implied."

"What's implied?" Emma asks hearing the tail end of our conversation, a blissful smile on her face. I love that I have a hand in putting it there. Ever since she told me her inner conflict, her eyes shine brighter and she carries herself with more sureness. Almost as if she is sharing the load a little, rather than sinking under its weight.

"That Arwen is the best foal," Alex jumps in and she smirks at his obvious attempt to distract her.

"True, but I know you're lying." Emma punches him playfully before running away as he chases her.

"As entertaining as this is, I need to go help Jesse finish up building the new round pens." Pulling Emma into my arms, I kiss her deeply, relishing in how much more relaxed she is around me. "I love you."

"I love you too." Reluctantly I release her and untie Charger.

Riding away, my face hurts from smiling so much. Hearing those three words for the first time was a dream come true and each time she says them after feels like a gift. In that moment there was a shift in our relationship, she entrusted me to be a person who would never hurt her. That trust means more to me than anything else in the world and I will cherish it always because she is my forever. There is no one else, never has been despite my feeble attempts to find it. Even when Natalie and I were dating, her disrespect for our relationship stung, but more due to my pride being hurt than actually feeling sad it didn't work. With Emma, my pride is set aside; all there is are my feelings for her and everything I will do to make her life good.

If I've learned anything in the past eleven months it's that our time here is short. It can be taken away at any time and that means we need to make the most of it.

Joining Jesse, we unload the boards that had been cut and pile them around the freshly pounded posts. Each round pen is built quickly once we find our rhythm and it's not long before I'm home and in the shower, eager to go on a date with Emma. Jesse asked what kinds of dates we had gone on today and I realized that I haven't taken her out officially yet. Everything we've done has been on the ranch.

I finish cleaning myself up and realize I didn't give Emma a heads up. This should be interesting.

> Me: I'm taking you out tonight. Be ready in half hour.

> Emma: I get an hour, Mr. Bossypants.

> Me: Bossypants? Lol

> Emma: Yes, because you're so bossy sometimes. Now shush so I can get ready.

Tossing my phone onto the bed chuckling, she hasn't seen just how bossy I can be. I'm grabbing clothes from my dresser, when Emma's photo catches my eye. It's the most recent picture I have of her, taken right before her parents' crash. Comparing the way she looked then to how she is now, I see the difference. Yet somehow, now that she has started therapy and begun to deal with her grief there is an air of hope around her. With hope comes healing and with healing comes the ability to really live. Setting the photo back down on my dresser, this time front and center, I quickly finish getting ready so I have time to complete the arrangements before picking her up, maybe it's a good thing I have an hour.

CHAPTER NINETEEN

Emma

Looking in my closet, I feel a little lost. I have no idea what to wear. I should have asked Dane what we're doing, but it's too late. I have ten minutes until my hour is up. Sighing, I throw on some dark wash jeans and a flowing strapless top. Finishing the look with a cute sweater, I grab my flip flops and head outside to sit on the porch swing. Excitement fills me as I wait; his demanding text was honestly a turn on and curiosity fills me at what he could possibly have planned.

The door to their house opens and I watch as Dane crosses the short distance to my house. He's dressed casually in jeans and a black t-shirt that hugs his body. Damn, he's so hot. Ever since I told him how I feel, there is a lightness to our relationship . . . a lightness to me that I didn't expect.

He takes the steps two at a time, striding purposefully towards me. Standing, I wrap my arms around him breathing in his soft cologne.

"You look beautiful." His lips graze my bare shoulder sending shivers down my spine and settling in my core. "I realized today that we have yet to go on a proper date. We haven't left the ranch except to run errands. Then I thought, who cares if we don't leave the ranch? This place fits perfectly with us." He smiles, his dimples popping out and grabs my hand leading me to the quad he has parked at the head of a trail I haven't explored since we were children.

Wrapping my arms around Dane, he takes off and we go flying down the trail. The lights from the quad guide the way, but in the darkness of the forest all else is shrouded in shadows as the sun sets. Closing my eyes, I rest my cheek against Dane's back enjoying the heat of his body contrasting with the cool air that blows around us. Being this close to him, I sigh in contentment at how happy I am. It had seemed impossible not too long ago, but I see the light at the end of the tunnel. It may be in the distance, but it's there.

Sitting up as we slow and come to a stop, my eyes widen as I look at Dane's treehouse for the first time in thirteen years. He has strung twinkle lights throughout the trees giving everything a magical quality. Light shines from inside the treehouse, curious as to what he has set up, I climb the ladder and crawl inside the small door. Moving to the side so Dane can follow me in, I feel how wide my eyes are as I look at the lanterns hanging from the hooks in the corners and the pile of blankets and pillows surrounding a cooler and picnic basket.

"This is perfect." Dane's smile is soft, loving, and reaches his eyes. Crawling over to him, I kneel in front of him smiling. "Way better than anything we could do in town." Tilting my head up, I kiss him softly before getting cozy in the mound of pillows. Dane sits down across from me and smirks when I frown at him.

He opens the cooler and hands me a bottle of water before

moving to the picnic basket. I watch his hands pull food out and my mouth waters. He passes me a toasted sandwich with chicken, guacamole, tomatoes, and alfalfa sprouts. Taking a bite, I groan at how delicious it is.

"That's why I sat over here. If I was right next to you, that sandwich would be out the window and you would be on your back." His light eyes darken with his words, looking at me with desire as he takes a bite of his own sandwich. My body heats up in anticipation and I teasingly lick my fingers clean. Dane narrows his eyes and devours his sandwich, wiping his fingers with a towel.

He crawls towards me, slowly like a lion hunting its prey, causing butterflies to explode in my stomach. His look, his intensity, the way he moves makes me wet and I freeze waiting to see what he will do.

Not breaking eye contact, he pushes all the food to the side and calmly takes the water bottle I'm gripping in my hand and throws it aside. Dane trails his fingers up my legs leaving a wake of tingles until he reaches my hips. Grabbing them gently, he lifts me into the center of the pillow mound.

Air rushes out of my lungs as my back hits the pillows, Dane leaning down towards me. Closing my eyes, I anticipate his kiss, but it never comes. Instead, I feel his gentle breath over my face as his fingers slide up under my shirt grazing my skin whisper soft.

Dane lifts my shirt up and I shift to allow him to pull it over my head. Unhooking my bra, he slides it off, continuing to glide his fingertips gently over my skin.

His head dips and his lips finally make contact with my skin as he lightly kisses my neck and shoulder. My head falls back, the teasing kisses flooding my senses as he builds the anticipation. My body burns and aches, my heart pounding with desire.

My back arches as he sucks a nipple into his mouth, teasing it with his tongue while his hands undo my jeans. Aching as he pulls away, I eagerly go to help him remove my jeans, but he pushes me hands away.

"Emma." His tone is firm, warning me. "Hands by your side." I do as he says, resisting disobeying him because all I want is for him to be inside me.

Gripping the pillows, I lift my hips as he removes the rest of my clothing. Hands sliding up my legs, he grips my hips and blows gently on me.

Whimpering as he kisses softly along my inner thighs, but not where I need him most.

Gasping as his tongue finally strokes me, I fist my hands in his hair pulling when he moves away.

"Hands down!" Words won't form as I grab the pillows. I guess I'm really getting Mr. Bossypants this evening.

He sucks my clit and thrusts two fingers into me, building me up until I can feel the brink of an orgasm. Pulling away, he smirks at the expression of frustration on my face.

Dane leans back, removing his clothes and crawling over top of me. He slides into me part way before pulling back out.

"What the hell? Stop being such a tease!" No longer able to be silent, I grab his hips and try to pull him back in.

He grips my wrists firmly in his hands and pins my arms above my head, teasing me. "We've already done that, we need to try something new. I have to find your favorite, remember?" Moaning as he flips me over and pulling my hips up, he thrusts into me. His pace is hard and fast, relentless, the position allowing him to push in deeper. Every nerve ending in my body fires as I come, clenching around him. Even lost in my own bliss the force of his orgasm brings me out of my haze as he thrusts into me one last time before pulling us down onto the pillows.

Dane's fingers stroke circles over my back as we look into each other's eyes. Every day with him makes me feel even more complete, more complete than I expected to feel without my family.

My eyes grow heavy as he rubs and I let sleep pull me in. It no longer scares me to go to sleep, instead I relish in the act of falling asleep with the man I love.

"I love you."

He brushes his lips over mine. "I love you too."

～

Dane

Stretching my arms above my head, I close my books and file them away. Thanks to Alex's website, I have training clients starting in September. The new arena expansion is booked and should be completed by then.

Sighing when the phone rings, I check the caller ID and quickly swipe my finger. "How did it go, man?"

Jesse's voice is quiet, but I can feel the fury over the phone. "Mom was fine. As predicted, Dad was a complete asshole. I need to move out."

"Oh shit. Do you need a place to stay?" Jesse was only staying there temporarily, but his father kicking him out is such a huge kick in the balls.

"I found one. A buddy of mine has an extra room and he said he had been thinking of getting a roommate."

"When are we going out? I will round up everyone."

"I do need to get out and have some fun. I'm just packing up what I can, my mom is going to send the rest of my stuff next week." Shuffling comes over the phone as I hear Jesse tape a box shut. "How about we meet at Linger in two hours? It will be before it gets busy and we should be able to grab a booth."

Emma and I arrive at Linger early to save a booth. It's her first time and when we stop outside, her hesitance makes me laugh.

"Trust me."

"I do, but right now I'm wondering if that's a smart decision. Am I going to be cut with a rusty knife?" There is laughter in her voice, teasing me.

Shaking my head, I link my fingers with her and open the door leading her inside. Standing to the side, I watch as she takes in the view. The soft lighting, cozy booths, and well-stocked bar. "Wow."

"See, it's just a disguise." She looks around as I guide her through the crowd to an empty booth. A server comes up and we order drinks. I get my usual Big Rock and Emma orders a long island iced tea.

Scanning the crowd, I'm relieved to see Yvette isn't here, but the night is still young.

"What are we drinking?" Lia, Ryan, and Alex join us, sliding into the booth. Emma passes her drink over to Lia who tries a sip. "Oh yeah! That's tasty."

"Holy shit." Emma's jaw drops as she looks at the door.

"Oh my." Lia follows Emma's gaze and watches as Jesse leads a guy to the table.

"Hey, guys. This is Ashton, I just moved into his place." Jesse and Ashton sit down as Emma and Lia gawk. Nudging Emma, I cock my eyebrow at her. She blushes and kisses me gently. Wrapping my arm around her, I chuckle as Lia openly checks out Ashton.

Alex looks between Lia and Ashton, a sullen look on his face as he downs his beer.

"What's going on there?" Emma looks over at Alex and giggles.

"I'm not sure yet, but whatever it is they're not as sneaky as they think they are." She smiles at Alex when he glances our way and then I notice that he purposely doesn't look Lia's way again. Huh. Interesting.

As the night progresses, it becomes glaringly obvious that Ashton is into Jesse. Lia picks up on that and moves her attention back to Alex. How did I miss the sparks between those two before now?

"Want to dance?" Emma nods as the DJ starts playing a slow song. I lead her onto the dance floor and wrap my arms around her. The warmth of her body pulls me in and I can't help but smile at her as she rests her cheek on my chest, closing her eyes.

Everything fades. The music. The people. The sounds of the bar. It's just me and her. The soft curves of her body molding to me, she is leaning on me letting me support her as we sway on the dance floor. The beat of my heart is steady and sure, there is no doubt in my mind this woman is mine to love forever.

The future I have envisioned for us is finally coming true and the feeling of knowing that her heart has finally caught up to mine is surreal. It's the best feeling in the world, but some nights as I fall asleep I wonder if I will wake up to find it was only a dream. Tilting my head down, I kiss her lips softly groaning as she deepens the kiss.

It's easy to forget we're in public when Emma kisses me and it's not until Alex's voice breaks through our bubble that I remember we have an audience. "Get a room! Song is over by the way." Alex's hand rests on Lia's elbow as he guides her off the dance floor, mocking us as Emma lifts her head and gives him the finger. She smiles at me and kisses me gently before we turn to head back to the table.

Meandering through the crowd, a woman with blonde hair and baby blue eyes blocks our path, it takes a moment for the fog of my dance with Emma to clear for me to realize it's Yvette. She is staring at Emma intently and fierce protectiveness floods my body at the disdainful expression she wears. Wrapping my arm even tighter around Emma, I clear my throat. Yvette drags her gaze away from Emma and her expression changes from disdainful to hungry. She really cannot hide the ugliness of her spirit any longer.

"Yvette, we would appreciate it if you would move." She steps to the side with a scowl and we walk silently to the booth, the daggers being thrown in our direction as we walk following us the entire way.

Sliding into the booth, Alex leans over when he sees Emma's face. Even though he whispers to her, I'm close enough to hear what he says. "Are you okay? You look like you're about to retreat back into yourself and we just got you out of that."

"I'm fine." Emma plasters on a smile, as she tunes in to the conversation our friends are holding. My eyes are fixed on her, everything tense as I gauge her mood and what could possibly be running through her mind. She slowly starts to relax, her smile becoming genuine and the tension leaves my body. I would be tense too if I ran into her coward of an ex-boyfriend, although that would probably lead to me punching the douche just because he's an idiot for letting Emma go.

We've had the previous relationship discussion. It wasn't as awkward as I thought it would be and my past didn't seem to bother her. I'm curious to find out what her reaction is now that she has met Yvette. I'm guessing it is a "What the fuck" reaction. Emma is sensitive to how people present themselves and she probably saw straight to Yvette's cold-hearted core. My gut is in knots and I glance out of the corner of my eye to where Yvette is at the bar flirting with her next victim. The look in her eyes was devious and I feel like I need to protect Emma from her. She doesn't look our way and I shake off the feeling. I'm just being paranoid.

Soon Emma, Jesse, Ashton, and I are the only ones left at the table.

"Guys, I just love you. Thanks for understanding and being there for me." Laughing as Jesse slurs his words, Ashton helps him out of the booth.

"I better get him home, before he is a complete dead weight."

"We're gonna go too. Let me help you." Pushing myself out of the booth, I lift Jesse's other arm over my neck. Emma walks behind us as we help him out the door and into Ashton's car. "Tell him he has the weekend off."

"Will do. It was nice to meet you." Ashton shuts the passenger door to his car and moves to the driver's side.

Yawning as we walk to my car, Emma leans into me. "You're a good friend."

"I don't care who he dates." My words come across more defensive than I intended, but her words surprised me. Emma stops and looks up at me, placing her hand on my chest.

"Obviously not. I meant paying for his drinks all night, supporting him to tell his dad when he was nervous to, and giving him time off during the busiest season to recover. It's the little things that count in friendship. Complete support and understanding. Giving when they are in need without expecting anything in return because you know if the roles were reversed, they would do the same for you. Those kinds of friendships are rare and it makes me love you even more when I see how much you cherish it." Her bright green eyes gaze up at me in admiration causing pride to fill me. That look in her eyes, I will do whatever it takes to keep that look there for the rest of our lives.

Bending down, I scoop her into my arms and twirl her around. Her laughter echoes through the parking lot and an older couple out for a walk smiles our way.

"Let's go home so I can have my wicked way with you." A smirk graces her face and she leans in sucking my earlobe between her teeth. Her hands wrap into my hair as she nuzzles my neck like when she thought she was dreaming. Picking up speed, I set her down by my car and lean her up against it, pressing my body into hers. "You keep that up and we won't make it home. In the car, now." Opening the door for her, I race to the driver's side to get home quickly. I need her. Now.

CHAPTER TWENTY

Emma

The sound of Dane's alarm going off rouses me from another dreamless sleep. Reaching my arm out from under the covers, I slap my hand around until I manage to shut it off. My body aches from last night and I smile at the memory of Dane's body against mine.

"I hate mornings." His voice is gruff and it sends shivers down my spine. Grumbling, he pulls the blanket over his head and buries his face into my side. It still surprises me that Dane has never adjusted to early mornings and it always makes my day being able to tease him just a little.

"You say that every morning. Come on, get up. Jesse will be waiting for you and I have to feed my critters before heading out to see Dr. Hughes. We bumped our appointments from Thursday afternoons to Monday mornings." Ripping the blankets off him, I laugh and jump away as he grabs for me. "Nope. No time for that this morning. Now get up."

"You're mean." Dane's pouty face is adorable and I can feel myself melting when Lia pounds on the door.

"Emma, your dog has been sitting on our porch for half an hour waiting for you."

Poor Chloe, she's not sure what to think on the nights I spend at Dane's. I haven't pushed having her come here when I spend the night because Johnathan couldn't stand Chloe. I don't really want to burst the blissful bubble we're in arguing over her.

"You know she is welcome to come sleep here too." Dane sees my guilt and automatically knows what I need to hear. "I know your ex didn't like her, but I adore that dog, she's pretty cool." Lunging into his arms, I kiss his face all over smiling like a fool. He makes me so happy.

Dr. Hughes added new paintings to the walls since I saw her last week. Remembering the look of pride that filled her face when I told her of my discussion with Dane, I can't wait to tell her that I also spoke to Lia and Ryan. My entire circle knows the full extent of what I've been dealing with and it feels as though a weight has been lifted off my shoulders.

We've also started working on managing my anxiety in the back seat of the car. Dr. Hughes had pointed out that everyone inadvertently was enabling my anxiety to cripple me and gave some suggestions on how to work through it. The challenges are still there, but it's been improving.

The side door of the room opens giving me a glimpse into her office as she comes in the door.

"Hello, Emma. You're looking well. How has the past week been?" As she sits in the chair next to me I fill her in on my conversations with Lia and Ryan.

"Oh, and we've been working with my anxiety and I have seen improvement. I know I have a long way to go, but I hope that one day it won't even be a thought." I never dreamt I would enjoy talking about my problems, I prefer to be there for everyone else and push mine aside, but therapy has been one of the best decisions I have made.

"That's wonderful. I know that the anniversary of your parent's passing is next week. August twentieth, I believe?" Her eyes are soft and she shifts to face me more directly as she asks about the date.

"Yes, that's correct. I know that this next week is going to be a challenge, but with the support of my friends and the strategies we have been working on, I'm not as anxious for it as I was. The sadness is there, but it's no longer crippling." My words are strong and sure. Dr. Hughes looks at me intently, and seems satisfied that I'm not covering up my emotions as I have done so much in the past. "I know it's hard to believe, I spent so much time locking everything inside, but I feel stronger. I'm not saying it will be easy, and I know I may need to remind myself. I guess I just have begun to realize that not only do I deserve better from myself, but so do my friends. I know Mom, Dad, and Grandpa would want me to be strong. I also feel confident that with Dane at my side I can get through anything."

Dr. Hughes crosses her legs and smiles at me. Trying not to fidget as she watches me, I reflect on my body and what it's telling me. Despite the looming date, my pulse is normal and I'm not sweating. There is no anxiety, no fear. The sadness is there, the longing to be able to talk to them and see them, but that will never disappear. Shockingly, I feel prepared to deal with it and I know that the strength I gain from Dane's love and support has a major part to play in my current mental state.

Dr. Hughes focuses the session on different coping mechanisms to help me get through the next couple of weeks; she's on vacation next week and is regretful that we won't be able to have a session. I make note of the tension releasing exercises, but the one that stands out the most is holding some sort of ceremony in their honor. Despite Grandpa passing away just under a month later I think I'll celebrate all three of them together.

When I get home, Lia is waiting for me for our weekly trail ride. Her horse, Ollie, is a gorgeous black gelding who has won several reining competitions. He is so smart and so kind; if I could I would steal him from her. He's patiently standing by my gate as Lia leads Chandler out, so I scratch him under his chin in his favorite spot.

"I hope you don't mind, but I had Alex saddle him up for you. I thought it would be nice to just head out." She swings up into her saddle and smiles at me as I give Chandler a hug. Slipping my boot in the stirrup, I grab the horn and pull myself into the saddle.

"Damn, he's so much taller than Serenity." I laugh as I adjust myself in the saddle.

Lia leads me down the path to where Arwen is now held, soon she will be able to come home and I can't wait.

"How was therapy today?" The trail opens into a field with rolling hills, Arwen standing out in the grass grazing amongst the other babies.

"It was good. Dr. Hughes was a little worried because she's away next week, but I think I'm going to do okay. The sadness is there, obviously, but I have the support from all of you and that makes it not so daunting."

"You better know that we're here for you! Seriously though, I'm glad to hear you sounding so confident, the changes in you from June until now has been immense. I'm really proud of you."

"Moving home was the best decision I could've ever made, even if I didn't know it at the time." We finish the ride along the fence to the gate in silence and Lia patiently waits while I give Arwen some carrots. Arwen follows along the fence until she can't anymore, whinnying after me as we continue away.

"She has grown so attached to you. I bet you're excited to take her home." Lia looks back at Arwen still staring in our direction and smiles.

"I can't wait! Alex is building a smaller pen next to the one the horses are in so she can slowly integrate into the herd. Dane says she can come home as soon as that's done." We ride chatting about the horses, Lia is going to keep the black colt to train.

"Are you going to teach Alex how to train?"

"I don't know that I'm the best teacher for that. If he wants to learn, he is more than welcome to help me though. You, Dane, or Ryan have more experience than I do." We turn into a treed part of the property that leads to an open field where we can let the horses go. As we wind through the path, Lia falls silent. Turning to look back at her, she has a pensive look on her face, almost dreamy. "Whatcha thinking about?" She jolts out of her thoughts and blushes at my teasing voice.

"Oh, ummm, I was thinking about when I finally get to train my colt. I'm struggling to think of a name for him, I know it will come to me, but I hate not being able to call him anything." Lia looks at me, a slight flush remaining on her cheeks and I laugh as she fiddles with the horn.

"You're a terrible liar, but I'll let you get away with it. When you're ready to tell me what the hell is going on with you, you will." The relief is evident on Lia's face that I'm willing to just let it go. It's so obvious that I decide to stop teasing her, something is clearly going on and I know I hate it when people push me.

Leading the way out of the trees and into the field, I kick Chandler into a canter, letting him go as we race across the field. This rush is amazing and while I laugh at the thrill running through my veins, I send a quick thank you to my grandfather for letting me come home. He could have sold his property to the Hyatts, but he chose to let me come back to where my heart has always truly been. As we slow down to an easy trot, Lia and Ollie blast past us before stopping and turning back.

"That never gets old." The wind blows our hair around our faces, our cowboy hats shielding our eyes from the sun. Gazing at the landscape, I breathe in the fresh summer air watching the grass wave in the breeze, the leaves rustling. "I was thinking of doing a memorial thing for my parents and Grandpa next week. I wish I could have it at their gravesite, but I don't feel right asking everyone to go there."

"Why weren't they buried closer to here?" The curiosity in Lia's voice is empathetic and I know she isn't asking to upset me. I wish they were closer, that was the one downside of moving back here. Leaving them behind.

"Dad's parents were both buried there and so they had planned for that too. Grandpa wanted to be close to Mom, so when they made that decision he asked in his will that his ashes be spread there." My heart squeezes with regret at not planning on going to see them, but I want my support network around me, my new family, and I know they can't up and leave.

"That makes sense." We sit silently, both reminiscing. "I meant to tell you that Mom and Dad are trying to make it home in time to be here for you next week. They said that another month is too long to be away from us kids." We laugh. I guess parents never stop being parents.

"Oh really? I can't wait to see them, it's been too long." Darren and Juliette never forgot me over the years, sending cards to celebrate birthdays, graduations and any other major events in my life. After the crash, they offered to fly up to help me with everything, but I told them no. I regret refusing them, I know it hurt, but I was not in the place to see them, quickly spiraling into the black hole that held me captive for almost a year. They attended both funerals, but I was like a shadow and don't even recall much of their short visit. The need to be present in the moment fills me and it is one more thing to help me get through next week.

Lia looks at her watch and sighs reluctantly. She gazes at the field longingly, but shakes her head and turns to look at me. "I had to book a client in this afternoon, we better head back."

"Okay, I wanted to surprise Dane with a visit before I get to work this evening." She smiles and we nudge our horses into a trot, they are eager to head home and eat so they keep up a quick pace the entire way back.

Closing the gate behind me, I notice a strange car in the drive. Dane has been having the odd meeting with potential clients for his training program. Faltering, I debate whether to surprise him or not but decide to pop in anyways.

Dane

Wiping my forearm across my face, I look at the round pens Jesse and I have finally completed. There are two smaller ones and one larger one. The larger one is the perfect size for round penning a more experienced horse, whereas the smaller ones are better for green horses.

"Damn, we made good time. Can you stay for a beer? I have a cooler I stocked before we left, hoping we would finish early." Jesse pulls his cap off, and wipes his face with his shirt.

"That sounds perfect, it's fucking hot out today." A gentle breeze is flowing, but it's not easing the heat of the sun. I pull a couple beers from the cooler and pop the caps. Handing Jesse the bottle, I take a deep swig before sitting on the back of the truck.

"How's it going living with Ashton?" Jesse hasn't said much about his abrupt move from his parents and into Ashton's, but I picked up on more than friendship at Linger.

"It's fine. Dad still won't talk to me, but Mom has come to visit. She likes Ashton and insists on setting us up. That woman is going to make me homeless if she keeps pushing."

"If you're interested in him why not go for it? I side with your mom." I thought discussing his relationships might be awkward or different, but in reality, it's just the same as if we were discussing my relationship with Emma. Smiling as I think about her, I can't help but contemplate all the things I get to do to her later.

"I'm his roommate nothing more." Jesse takes in the goofy smile on my face and smirks. "Thinking about Emma?"

"Always. She and Lia are probably setting out for their ride now. Oh, while I'm thinking of it I was hoping you would help Alex and me build a pen for Arwen attached to the corral her horses are currently in. I want to surprise her by bringing Arwen home sooner than she expects."

"Of course. I adore Emma, she is a sweetheart." Emma invited Jesse over for dinner the Sunday after we went to

Linger and they hit it off. Emma got a kick out of how Jesse calls me out on my shit and he got a kick out of how one look from Emma and I'm a puddle. "I've never seen you like you are with her. She truly is the missing link from your life."

"Yes, she is. It took me long enough to crack through her defense mechanisms though! I need to ask one more favor. Next week is the one year mark of when her parents died, do you think you can look after the day to day chores for me? I want to be as available as possible for her." I know Emma won't want me to stop everything for her, but she will need to deal with it. With Jesse's help, I can take the time off and just be there for her.

"Of course." We toss our empties back into the cooler and start packing up our tools. Shoving them into the box of the truck, we drive home.

"Okay, well, I'll see you tomorrow." Jesse takes off. Looking over, I see that Chandler is still gone so I head inside to shower and work on my schedule. The new training arena is complete and I have the walk through tomorrow just to make sure everything is exactly how I want it. My first client should be arriving the first week of September and I want everything to be perfect.

Instead of holing myself up in the office, I lay out my calendar and notes in the living room. I hate this part, trying to schedule my time so everything that needs to get done in the day is accomplished.

I grab water, chips, and guacamole to eat while trying not to pull my hair out. Thank goodness for Jesse, he's agreed to take over the afternoon feeding so I can focus on training all afternoon. Mornings will be regular chores and reserved for my own horses.

I'm sitting trying to figure out all the projects we need to accomplish before the snow flies when there is a knock on the door. Sighing in relief, I stretch and make my way to answer. My mind is reeling from trying to figure out how to fit everything and the distraction is welcome.

Opening the door, Yvette's smiling face greets me. Never mind, it's not welcome.

"Yvette." My tone is cold and her smile falters a bit before she plasters it back on her face.

"Aren't you going to invite me in?" Her voice is sugary sweet and it makes me feel sick to my stomach.

"I wasn't planning on it." Crossing my arms, I block the door. Her fake smile remains in place, her eyes hardening at being denied so bluntly.

"C'mon, it's so hot out here. I just wanted to talk to you about something." She shifts her voice into an irritating baby voice and it makes me want to gag.

"Fine. You get ten minutes." I'm being generous with my time, if I've learned anything about Yvette it is that she is rarely up to anything without self-gain. She has nothing to gain here so I'm wary of what the hell she wants.

"I was offered a job in Vancouver and came to say goodbye." Taking a step back from where she stands, I examine her closely. She doesn't appear to be lying, but I don't really understand why she felt the need to inform me of this.

"Congrats. It wasn't necessary to stop by to tell me that." It sounds cold, but this woman has been driving me insane for months and the thought of being rid of her fills me with relief.

"I realize that." Her voice is sharp and she takes a deep breath in, shifting her voice back to her fake sweet voice with her fake smile. "I also came to apologize for my behavior, I'm not used to being told no and I realize I've been pretty pushy."

Narrowing my eyes at her, I watch her carefully. Despite her words, her eyes lack sincerity and I take another step back, hitting the wall behind me. Shit. "Well, what's done is done. I think you've said what you need to say. Good luck in Vancouver."

Yvette closes the space between us until she stands barely a foot away from me. "I still have one other thing I want to say."

CHAPTER TWENTY-ONE

Emma

Bounding up the steps to Dane's, I smile as I pause at the door; I haven't been this happy since before my parents' death. Turning the handle, I swing the door open ready to call out a greeting. My smile falters and I freeze.

Yvette stands in front of Dane, hand pressed on his chest. His face is tilted towards her, his eyes on hers. The pose is intimate and shock fills me before my reflexes catch up to what my brain is processing.

A gasp slips out of my mouth, my hand slaps over my lips as his head jerks up to meet my gaze in surprise. Unable to take in the sight before me, tears flood my eyes as I spin on my heel and run out of the door.

Go back. You're misreading the situation.

Maybe I'm not.

How will I know if I don't go back?

I can't right now.

Faintly, through the pounding in my head, I think I hear Dane call my name, but I run faster. I can't face him right now, too destroyed by the fact he let her get that close to hear him out. Flinging the gate open to the horses, I swing up onto Serenity's bare back, my hands fisting in her mane and I crouch low as I kick her into a canter. Together we race out of the pen, I'm so angry and hurt that I don't stop to close the gate before heading down the long driveway. The same driveway that just under two and a half months ago brought a sense of relief, now is too long in my attempt to escape.

Fuming sobs wrack my body and as we leave the driveway and turn onto the road, I slow Serenity to a trot, holding her mane and shaking. Serenity prances, unsure what to think of my current state and lack of direction.

Breathe in. Hold for ten. Breathe out.

The sound of tires coming from the driveway brings me back, my heart pounding as I nudge Serenity back into a canter. A gap in the trees catches my attention and relief hits me momentarily. Quickly turning off the road, I start up an old, long forgotten trail and finally slow to a walk.

Laying on Serenity's back, I let her come to a stop as my tears fall with the broken pieces of my heart. Why would he let her in the house when he knows what she's after? A little voice in the back of my head tells me I'm wrong to be so upset, that I should have stayed, but I push that voice aside.

Clutching my hands to my chest as my heart pounds, the physical hurt causes guttural cries to echo in the trees. Lungs burning as I fight for air, eyes blurry from the tears as I cry into Serenity, I try to remember to breathe.

I know I'm blowing this out of proportion, but the emotional part of my brain has taken over the rationale one. Her hand was on his chest. After everything she's done, why would he let her get that close?

Serenity grows restless, so I nudge her to keep moving. My eyes are swollen to little slits, my mind reels with a frenzy of emotion.

The other shoe dropped. Bad things come in threes. This is the third thing.

Letting my guard down was the hardest thing I have done and this is what happens. My chest physically hurts from the smashing of my heart and it feels like I've been punched in the gut. I'd been doing so well. I thought I had it under control. He said he was there for me no matter what.

My hands loosen on her mane and I pay little attention to where we're going, letting her walk on her own free will. I didn't realize it was possible for my heart to feel more pain than it has already endured, but it feels as though my entire soul has shattered. My whole body hurts. I didn't realize it was possible for your entire body to break. It's not just my heart that aches. It's my head, lungs, stomach . . . All the way down to my toes.

Serenity jumps to the side, acting skittish. Instead of looking up where I'm going, I nudge her to keep moving forward, drowning in my sorrow.

Serenity rears up, I barely glimpse the buck as it disappears, my body is flying off her back. My leg smacks into a tree —hard. My arms fly out to block the fall, and a loud crack echoes through my body as I land on my arm. I didn't even have a chance to process what was happening until I'm in a heap on the ground.

Gasping as I clutch my left arm into my chest. The pain is severe and I know something is broken. Putting weight on my left arm is out of the question, and my leg throbs from the impact on the tree. Physical pain from the fall is a welcome pain from the emotional void I am stuck in, especially since I know I'm overreacting and can't seem to shut it down. Physical pain is easy to handle. I have no more tears to cry, so dry sobs heave out of my body while I attempt to block out the internal ache and focus outside of myself. I could do it once, I can do it again.

The blackness that has been hiding in the corners of my mind comes creeping out, engulfing me and I succumb to the familiarity. Serenity pushes me with her nose, unwilling to leave my side, her soft presence trying to bring me back. Turning away from her gentle gaze, I close my eyes and mentally harden myself.

Pushing the emotions away, I welcome the dark. I welcome the familiarity of ignoring how I feel. It helped me survive before and it will help again. This time I know better, I know better than to push it away. There is no light anymore, the little hope I held onto for almost a year is extinguished as I enfold myself into the cold embrace of darkness.

When I wake, fresh tears greet me and despite my attempts to numb myself from the heartache, its presence lingers.

Gazing around me, I notice that the light of the forest is changing as the sun sets.

Taking a deep breath, I try to stand, but cry out at the pain in my body. My entire left side feels bruised and even if I can stand long enough, there is no way I can get on Serenity without help. Leaning my back against the tree, I regret leaving my phone at home and settle in for a long night of watching the stars twinkle at me as though I didn't have my world shattered a matter of seconds.

My mind is numb when I think back on what I witnessed. How could Dane do that? I wouldn't invite Johnathan inside, I would send him away. In that brief moment, I realized just how much Dane can hurt me. Why were they so intimately posed? My gut feels off, but I push it away, favoring the blackness to anything else. The numb world, the world of not dealing that is where I feel comfortable. I knew everything else was too good to last. These things come in threes and that was it. Why not? Why not have everything that brings me happiness torn away from me.

Not everything. That little voice attempts to bring reason again and it's stronger, not letting me shove it away even though I'm trying. The light I had extinguished tries to flicker as something Dr. Hughes said in our last session crosses my mind.

Even when it feels all has been lost, remember those that stood by your side. Remember those that look down on you and even if you can't see them, remember to FEEL them in your heart.

It's too much. The flickering light is extinguished as I fight for something, the wrong thing. Numbness. This time I won't let it go.

Closing my eyes, I succumb to the darkness again.

Rustling rouses me from my fitful sleep and I pry my eyes open when I feel a cold nose and warm body wiggling around me. Chloe stands in front of me, stubby tail wagging and with a cry I wrap my right arm around her. Of course she would find me.

"Oh, thank God, Emma!" Looking up, I see Alex's worried face. Even though I know I should feel some sort of emotion, I continue to allow the detachment I've embraced keep its hold on me and his face shifts from worried to scared. "What the hell happened? Dane . . ."

"Don't. I can't deal with thinking about him right now." Tears threaten again and I steel myself. The stone fortress rebuilding itself around me. "I need your help, I have to go to the doctor." My voice is hoarse and raw, Alex's eyes flare at the sound as he bends down to lift me, cursing when I cry out.

Holding me in his arms, he clucks his tongue at Serenity

and the four of us make our way to the road. The walk is long and it shocks me how far I had gone into the trail.

"Please don't let Dane see me." Whispering, I meet the concerned gaze of his hazel eyes and whatever he sees makes him nod. Setting me down on a fallen tree, he pulls out his phone and sends someone a text.

I'm in a daze as Alex's truck pulls up and Lia hops out. My mind is no longer in the present. Whatever changes that have occurred to me since being here fight against the numbness I seek.

I want the numbness.

No, I don't.

Back and forth until the numbness finally wins. For now. I need it for right now.

"She doesn't want Dane to know anything. I'm not sure what happened, but I need to take her to the hospital." I feel their eyes on me, but I try not to care as I teeter on the fallen tree. Alex scoops me into his arms, cringing as I cry out. Lia's gasp breaks through the weak barrier my mind has put together and I look at her. It hurts so much.

"I've got Chloe and Serenity." Lia puts on Serenity's halter and tries to snap a leash on Chloe. She jumps away, whimpering at Alex's feet.

"Chloe stay." The words that come out of me don't sound like me. They are quiet, broken, and void of emotion. Chloe sits and lets Lia snap the leash in place, whimpering as Alex loads me in the truck and drives away.

~

Dane

. . .

Yvette lifts her hand and rests it on my chest. Clenching my hands into fists, I look down at her, annoyance filling me that she is pulling this shit and I was stupid enough to let her in the house. Her expression is smug as she looks up at me.

A soft gasp startles us and I snap up my head to meet the anguished gaze of Emma standing in the doorway. Her hand slaps over her mouth and she bolts out the door.

Pushing Yvette aside, I lunge for the door. "Emma!" She keeps running and I turn on Yvette in a rage. "Get. The. Fuck. Out. Of. My. House." My voice is soft, deadly, and she bolts out the door with me on her heels only to see Emma bareback on Serenity disappearing down the driveway. Looking over at her house, I see the gate to the horse pen is open and run to close it before Belle and Chandler escape and I lose precious time trying to round them up.

Racing to my truck, I spin around and speed down the driveway. Fuck, which way could she have gone? Turning right, I drive and drive before turning back and going the other way. I speed dial Alex.

"Hey, man, what's up?" His voice is chill. He has no idea.

"Ummm, do you know where Emma is?"

"No, and her phone is on the counter. I just looked out the window and Serenity is gone. They probably went to see Arwen again." Hanging up, shame fills me at my deception. There is no way that I could explain the situation to him. Dread fills me as I realize the chances of finding Emma in my truck while she is on horseback are slim.

Fuck.

"Dane?" Alex's voice is filled with curiosity at why I'm calling him again so quickly.

"I need your help. Emma walked in on something, took it the wrong way, and ran off on Serenity. Bareback and upset. I have no idea how to find her. Please, find her." Alex mumbles something about me getting castrated if I fucked up, but I will take that. Alex's first priority will always be Emma and in this moment, I just want her found.

It's getting dark when I finally ride Charger up to the barn and set him loose in his pen. I quickly gave up on driving and moved to horseback, but the vast number of trails going in and out of our property make it near impossible to find her. Worry fills me as I fight to stay calm. I need to fix this.

Anger fills me, I broke my promise and that is something I can never take back. Why was I such an idiot? I fucking know better. Yvette better damn well be moving to Vancouver, otherwise there will be hell to pay. I'm betting if she wasn't, she is now after being kicked out of my house.

Emma's house is dark, but Serenity is back in with the other horses. My feet pound across the gravel and I'm soon beating on the door. No movement from inside.

"They're not here." Jumping at Lia's voice, I turn and see her silhouette on the porch swing. Her tone is angry and I'm guessing Emma filled her in.

"Where did they go? Lia, I need to talk to her." Desperation fills me as I plead with her and I'm not above getting on my knees and begging.

"I'm not telling you. I promised Alex." Lia's jaw is set.

"What about Emma, did you promise her?" I sit next to Lia on the porch swing, flinching when she moves away from me.

"Emma could barely get two words out. She was destroyed. What the fuck happened?" Her voice vibrates and I don't think I've ever seen this kind of anger directed towards me. In fact, I've only ever seen Lia this angry at one person and we don't discuss Graham—ever.

"Yvette came by . . . Ouch!" I rub my arm, grimacing as the sting of Lia's smack. "Will you stop and listen?"

"Fine. But if you ruined this over that freak, I'm going to cut off your dick."

"Yvette came by to tell me she is moving to Vancouver. I told her off and she said she wanted to apologize for her behavior. The next thing I know, I'm backed against the wall because the woman has no personal space and her hand is on my chest. Emma walked in on that and got the wrong idea. It was a déjà vu moment, except worse." Relief fills me as the rage in Lia deflates and she slumps against the back of the swing. It's short-lived though as I see the look of a broken-hearted Emma play over and over in my head.

"Oh shit." Dread fills me as she sits there in silence. She looks up at me, anger glinting as she scowls and hits me again. "You're a fucking idiot. I can't believe you would let that woman into our house." Regret. Shame. Anger. They all fight for first place as my head spins. Have I lost the love of my life over my own stupidity?

"Lia, where are they?"

"Dane, I promised Alex I wouldn't say anything and I intend on keeping that promise. You're going to have to go through him and then figure out a way to get through to her. She's in lock down." Lia stands and squeezes my shoulder, hard. Flinching as she looks at me I drop my head into my hands. "I don't even know what to say to you, that was just really stupid. I'm disappointed that she was able to manipulate you." She walks away and I watch her as she crosses the yard and enters the house without a backwards glance.

Disappointment doesn't even begin to describe the emotions running through me.

CHAPTER TWENTY-TWO

Emma

We finally leave the hospital at three in the morning. I've been X-rayed, poked, prodded, plastered, and drugged. Oh, the drugs. The numbness from the morphine they gave me to help with the pain is blissful.

Alex is driving, periodically glancing at me out of the corner of his eye. Ignoring him, I stare out the window, my left arm nestled against my chest in the brace the doctor put it in. Sitting in the emergency room for several hours, having to see the concerned look in Alex's eyes was almost as painful as the damage done to my body.

"Emma, are you going to tell me what happened?" Alex's voice cracks through the fortress I've rebuilt and I know I can't keep him out. I've spent two months trying not to be that girl anymore and somewhere along the way I managed to succeed. I've been attempting to ignore the strength I've found within but it's exhausting staying in the numbness, embracing the dark, when I've fought to come back to the light. I've been fighting my weakness and that part of me wants to continue to fight.

Sighing, I look at Alex. He's been there for me through it all. I can't block him out, I won't let myself. "I walked in on Yvette and Dane. He was against the wall and her hand was on his chest. I didn't stick around to see what else was about to go down." My voice cracks as I try to keep it void of emotion. I may not be the as weak as I was, but I'm still fighting for strength. The darkness wants to engulf me and part of me wants to let it. Pain doesn't exist as long as I stay here, well at least I can pretend it doesn't; even if I'm tired of pretending.

"Are you sure you didn't misinterpret what you saw?" Alex speaks to me softly, cautiously. He knows how fragile I am right now, yet his words are like a boot stomping on the pieces of my shattered heart.

"It possible, but he still let her in the house. He still let her press him against the wall. And even if I'm misinterpreting the situation, it didn't look like he was doing much to remove her." Closing my eyes, I shut him out and clench my fists as he sighs with sadness. I've been fighting the little voice inside that has been saying the same thing. Anger at Dane is easier than anger at myself for still not being strong enough to stay and fight.

I need to constantly battle for myself, I don't want to battle for everything else too.

Maybe it's when you battle for something else that your true inner strength will start to win against yourself. I hate that little voice. She's a know it all bitch and shove her out of my head.

I'm startled awake as pain shoots through my body. Crying out, my eyes pop open and I'm met with Alex's grim expression.

"Sorry, Em, I was hoping the pain killers would prevent this from hurting so much. Can you walk?" Nodding, I plant my right foot on the ground and grip Alex's hand with mine. Teeth clenching, I tenderly put weight on my left leg. It hurts. Tears threaten to fall as I take my first step.

"Holy shit, Emma!" Looking up, I see Lia behind Alex. He must have called her. "What's the damage?" She's looking at Alex, not me. Part of me is annoyed that she doesn't ask me, but then again, I'm grateful to avoid more questions. Always torn in two directions.

Hobbling away from them, shoulders hunched, I just want to curl up in bed and sleep the next week away. Can't I have a rest before I start fighting to be better, this time without Dane by my side to help ease the weight?

"Her wrist is broken. The entire left side of her body is bruised from the impact. She flew into a tree and landed on that side. Her wrist broke because of its position when she tried to brace herself." Their eyes sear into my back as I slowly walk away, not really paying attention to anything but crawling into my bed. My foot slips on a rock and I cry out as I start to fall. Rolling away from my left side, I land on my right the jolt sending shooting pain throughout my body.

"Fuck!" Tears start as I lay on the ground, Lia and Alex crouched around me.

"Dammit! Emma, just let me help you!" Alex's voice is harsh and I cry harder, curling into myself.

"Dude." Lia scolds Alex. She turns away from him, her expression changing to one of empathy. "Come on, Em, I will help you get ready for bed." Alex picks me up off the ground for the second time in twenty-four hours and Lia leads us into the house. Normally I would be embarrassed, but by this point in the day, I guess I should expect it.

Once inside, she helps me change, cringing every time I cry out in pain and apologizing for every flinch and every whimper. "Lia, it's fine. The physical pain is easy to manage."

Finally, I'm in shorts and a tank top, tucked in bed with Chloe by my side.

"I know that you want to shut down, I see the struggle in your eyes and I understand why. Emma, please resist. You've made so much progress and things will work out." Lia pleads with me but I can't think about anything but escaping just for a little while. I should tell her I am resisting. That my mind no longer allows me to fully shut down no matter how hard I try, but I'm too tired. Letting the heaviness in my eyes pull them closed, I fall asleep without responding.

~

Dane

My bedroom door slamming open wakes me from a restless sleep and I sit up to a seething Alex. He stalks over to me, pulls his elbow back and punches me with a mean right hook. As soon as I saw him, I knew what was coming. I deserve it.

"If you need to, hit me again." Standing, I face him straight on and wait.

"You deserved that one, but I think another is uncalled for. How could you let that nut job into your house? You're the one who warned us about her and then you invite her in? What are you going to do to fix this?" Crossing his arms, he cocks his eyebrow and looks at me expectantly.

"I know. I'm an idiot. I'm still working on how to fix this, any suggestions?" Pursing his lips, he shakes his head. That has been the consensus of the day. I'm on my own to fix this mess. "I'm guessing you're here because you found her."

"I did."

"How is she?"

"Honestly, if I didn't know that you're innocent in all this I wouldn't tell you, but you're just an idiot." As he shares the information, horror fills me. Legs weak, I sit on my bed as he goes into detail after detail about bruises, a broken wrist, and the emptiness fighting to return. The only hope I have is that Alex said as much as she tried to shut down, it never quite reached her eyes.

"I can't believe I did it again. I promised I wouldn't."

"A good start would be setting some boundaries with people you know aren't trustworthy. You're a grown ass man. Secondly, don't make promises you can't keep." With that Alex leaves my room.

By the time Jesse meets me outside of Emma's house, I've already laid out the lumber and pounded the posts in. There has been no movement from her window and despite my hopes that she would come and talk to me, I know it's going to take more than me hanging outside of her house to get through to her.

"Shit, did you even sleep last night?" Jesse's eyes scan my face, taking in the bags under my eyes from tossing and turning all night. Jesse doesn't know what happened with Emma and I'm too ashamed to tell him.

"Not really." It's not fair to him, but I am miserable. My tone is all business and instead of continuing mindless chatter we get to work.

The new pen is finished within a couple of hours and Arwen is now exploring her new space. Out of the corner of my eye, I see Alex helping Emma down the porch and to the car.

She is favoring her left leg and the white of the cast on her left wrist peeks out from her sleeve. Even from a distance, I can see the pain in her eyes. Her head snaps up and she stares in my direction as I take a step towards them. Agony fills her face before she quickly hardens into a look of indifference and turns away, getting into the passenger side of Alex's car.

It hurts that she doesn't trust me enough to question what she saw, but I try to remind myself that she's still healing from past hurts. Maybe they have nothing to do with me, but they still impact how she sees the world.

"All right, what the hell is going on?" Jesse moves to stand in front of me, arms crossed in front of him and his best stern face glaring at me. Running my hand through my hair, I lean against the fence and watch Arwen. The words begin to flow and he stands there silently, listening. A muscle ticks in his jaw when I tell him how I let Yvette into the house, but he doesn't say anything.

"I don't even know what to say to you, man. It doesn't make sense that you would even let her in, let alone invade your personal space. You need to stop being so nice." Shaking his head, he walks away.

Pushing off the fence, I head to the house pausing as I step inside at the sound of Lia and Ryan talking.

"She really wants to go to their gravesite, but feels it would be an imposition on everyone." Hope finds its way into my shame as I realize they are talking about Emma. Creeping closer, I listen to see if I can figure something out to fix this.

"Why would she think that?" Ryan is so concrete about his dedication to people he cares about that it would never even register for him to consider it an imposition to fly to British Columbia for a memorial.

"It's far, plus all the animals. She wanted all of us there."

Pushing into the kitchen, Lia and Ryan both narrow their eyes at me and shake their heads. "Seriously? Enough is enough. I get that I fucked up by trusting Yvette, but are you going to punish me and in the process punish Emma? Or are you finally going to realize the sooner you help me the sooner she won't be hurt anymore?" I accepted their anger, justified it even, but knowing what Emma wants and that we can give it to her. That is more important.

"Damn, he's right. What are we doing? Besides, Emma can dish out punishment as she sees fit." Ryan grins at his last remark.

It's time to get to work. I need to make this right.

CHAPTER TWENTY-THREE

Emma

"Good morning, Sunshine." Alex laughs as I stumble into the kitchen and hands me a cup of coffee. Five days have passed since my accident and I'm no longer limping. The bruises have faded from a deep purple to a hideous yellow green. Soon the only trace of what happened will be the cast on my wrist and the broken pieces of my heart. "I figured we were still boycotting breakfast, so it's in the oven."

"Just until after Tuesday. Dr. Hughes said to tackle one thing at a time, and my parents' memorial takes precedent." Alex tracked down Dr. Hughes after the first three days of me being near comatose as I battled internally with how to deal with what I saw. At one point I screamed for Alex to hire a realtor; that we were selling and moving far away.

After that crazy moment he made me sit down for a Skype therapy session. It really helped, and while the pain is still there I have a functioning and somewhat rational brain again.

"Are you sure it's a good idea for us to go see them? What about everyone else?"

Yesterday Dane had stopped by as he has every day since he built Arwen's pen and I avoided him, leaving Alex to fend him off. Alex found me curled up on the couch, arms wrapped around Chloe and suggested we take off to do what I really want and that is to see them.

"Yes! Now, stop worrying that's all taken care of." He looks at me and I brace myself for what's next. It's the same every morning. "When we get back, what are you going to do about Dane? He isn't going to give up and that says a lot."

"I know, he's persistent. And I don't really know." Alex opens his mouth to speak, but I cut him off. "I know what you think and I've taken it into consideration. I'm processing." Everyone has told me to talk to him.

Talk.

Talk.

Talk.

I know this. I'm not stupid, I should've stayed and kicked her ass and then his before listening to him. Yet my flight instinct took over. I'm not overly proud and now I'm mostly embarrassed. Hindsight is twenty-twenty yet it doesn't strip away what seeing him pressed against that wall with her hand running down his chest did to my heart.

"Emma, you need to listen to me. You know Dane would never betray you. He made a mistake letting her in the house, but that's it. I know you don't want to hear it, but you're putting something on him because you're scared to fully let yourself be happy. Stop running away, be a grown ass woman, and talk to him." Alex has a solid grip on my arms, his tone firm.

My head falls, shoulders slumping. He's absolutely right. I'm being immature, "I know. I'm not thinking clearly. Can I just pass it off as the stress of the upcoming anniversary of my parents' death?"

"No. You can't. Now, I've booked our flight to Vancouver and the car is rented. We should be set to be there for early in the afternoon." He gives me a stern look.

"Thanks, Alex."

"Thanks, Alex what?" Lia walks in and gives me a hug. "I heard breakfast was in the oven and thought it might be nice not to cook."

"Emma and I are flying to Vancouver on Monday." Alex pulls out a breakfast casserole from the oven, quickly serving Lia and I as we drool over the delicious aroma.

"Oh my God! This is so good." Lia groans as she takes a bite out of Alex's concoction and I barely resist laughing at the look he gives her. She continues on, oblivious to him until he leaves the room. "What the hell?" We flinch as he slams his door.

Covering my mouth as I continue to hold in my laughter, tears flowing down my cheeks. "I think he is a little . . . ummm . . . sexually charged." Her eyes widen as she processes what I'm getting at and she blushes.

"Well, he better take care of that." Lia picks up her fork and silently starts to eat again, watching me from the corner of her eye. Thankful for the break in my own drama, I contemplate teasing her, but instead I decide to see if my hunch is right.

"I'm not really hungry, I'm going to go run with the horses and play with Arwen." Getting up, I put my breakfast in the fridge and slip into my boots. Chuckling to myself about Lia and Alex pretending their chemistry doesn't exist, I walk right into Dane as I turn from shutting my door. The impact on my wrist sends shooting pain up my arm and black spots fill my eyesight. Cradling my arm into my chest, I clench my jaw and fight the urge to cry.

"Shit, Emma, I'm sorry. You should sit down." Dane's voice is soft, gentle, and sends pangs right into my gut.

"I'm fine, really. I need to go." Avoiding his gaze, I scoot around him and run to my horses. The echo of his sad sigh replaying over and over.

Watching him from the corner of my eye, I see him ride away on Charger. Berating myself for being a coward, I start jogging to clear my head.

Am I being unreasonable? I believe Alex and Lia when they say nothing happened. In that moment, my fears and my anxiety got the best of me, but as I dwell on it, I know I overreacted. As much as I want to talk to him, to move past it . . . I'm embarrassed. I'm ashamed that I'm not as strong as I once was. How could he let her in and how could I not defend what I love?

A nudging in my back brings my awareness to my surroundings. I'm no longer running and Arwen is standing behind me. Wait? What?

"Pretty girl. How did you get in here?" Cooing, I stroke her neck and examine the fence. It's still intact. "Oh boy. You're going to be a fence jumper."

Grabbing some brushes, I make the rounds and play with my horses. They help bring a calmness I've been needing lately. The nightmares have continued to get better, despite everything, yet during the day I have periods where I can barely breathe. I know it's from trying to suppress my feelings, compartmentalize them into neat boxes when nothing is neat and tidy about the tirade of emotions I feel constantly. Regret, embarrassment, anger, sadness, even happiness at times. It's exhausting trying to keep up with myself.

Looking to the sky, I search for a feeling, a sign that my parents and Grandpa might be listening. "I miss you all so much. I want to be able to talk with you, rejoice with you. Why were you taken from me so soon? I don't have my shit together like I thought I did." My hand stills as I speak.

"Sometimes the bad needs to happen to make room for the good." Spinning at the familiar voice, a joyful sob breaks out of my chest at the sight of Juliette standing on the other side of the fence. Dropping the brush, I run to her and climb the fence.

Walking into her open arms feels like piecing part of me back together. "Where is Darren?" My voice is muffled, my face buried into her. Comfort washing over me as I enjoy her embrace.

"He is smacking some sense into that son of ours." Juliette's protective voice makes me laugh.

"Can he give him a couple extra for me?" Her laugh is like honey, soft and sweet.

"Now, let me look at you." She pushes me gently away and scans me, a frown lighting her face. "Well, despite your accident, you look better than the last time I saw you."

"I'm sorry about that . . ." Guilt. It's always there.

"Darling, you need to learn it is okay to struggle. It's okay to protect yourself, but you ever pull away from us like that again and there will be consequences." Her voice is stern and I nod meekly.

Smiling, I climb back into the pasture and collect my brushes. "I know. I'm seeing a therapist and it's helping." Admitting to that gets easier every time, especially when the look of support is there instead of pity.

"I'm glad. Well, I need to round up my children. I hear you're going back out to B.C. so make sure you come over for dinner when you get back." Juliette gives me a final squeeze and I'm glad that Alex talked me out of listing this place.

"I will."

My suitcase sits on the hotel room bed, open. Clothes are strewn over the bed, some onto the floor, and a few chucked across the room.

August 20th. One year since I lost my parents. A month before my grandfather passed away. The day that my world went spinning out of control. I'm not ready for today.

"Emma. Deep breaths. What you wear doesn't matter." Alex's voice is calm and placating.

"Yes, it fucking matters. I don't know why it does. I know it makes no sense, but it absolutely matters." He grabs my hands in his and pulls me into a hug. His arms are tight, exactly what I need to help release the tension.

"Okay. Okay." The warmth of his hug helps calm me a bit.

"Can you pick for me? I can't do it." He releases me and looks through my clothes. "I'm so stupid, I want Dane here and I spent so much time avoiding him. He quit coming by, I would be tired of trying too."

Alex gives me his big brother glare and hands me a simple black sleeveless dress. It has a subtle scoop neckline, and sits around my knees. It's perfect. "Emma, you reacted in the moment. There is no right or wrong in those situations. As for the rest of it, just deal with it day by day. Let's get through today first."

Taking the dress from him, he rests a hand on my shoulder and looks at me compassionately. Giving him a small smile, I close myself into the bathroom and get ready.

∼

Dane

. . .

Holy shit. It's been a whirlwind trying to get this set up, but we accomplished it.

Emma's family's gravesite is on the outer edge of the graveyard, and it has been decorated with an assortment of calla lilies, baby's breath, and morning glories.

The enclosed gazebo intended for gatherings such as these is set up with tables of food, more flowers, and soft twinkly lights behind sheer curtains.

Alex told me that Emma was not happy with the funeral. She had hoped it would be more of a celebration of life. That is what she's going to get. We all chipped in to make this everything she had hoped. Alex created a slideshow and each of us is going to give our favorite memories of William, Ben, and Katie. Mom and Lia cooked amazing treats. Dad and Ryan made a rustic picture frame and we all contributed to the photos now encased in it.

The selection of guests is exactly what Emma wanted, close and intimate.

Checking my phone for the time just as it vibrates with a text.

Alex: We're on our way.

Me: Okay. Should I leave?

Alex: No.

Hope fills me as I walk around everything one final time. It was hard to leave without fixing things with Emma, but this is more important.

The sound of gravel crunching under car tires alerts us to their arrival. Mom hooks her arm in mine and walks out with me. I'm proud as I examine the close group of people here to remember three wonderful people. Alex told me to keep it to my family and Jesse if he could come. We added Ashton as he has begun to spend time with our group as well.

The seven of us stand, waiting for Emma and Alex. And the look on her face as she takes us in is priceless. Shock is replaced by a shaky smile that she graces each of us with, even me. Alex holds her hand as they walk up to us and she is enveloped in a group of people who love her unconditionally.

"I can't believe you're all here. This is exactly what I wanted. Thank you." Emma's voice caresses my heart and all I want is to pull her into my arms. Holding myself back, I bask in the smile she sends my way before her attention is returned to someone talking to her. That one smile fills me with hope.

"We should get started. Emma, I know you had prepared something to say to your family. Would you like us to wait inside while you do that or do you want our company?" Mom steps in and gets us back on track.

"You can stay. I'm going to do this right this time." Tears already thicken her voice. I move to stand next to Lia, fisting my hands to resist the urge to wrap my arms around Emma.

"It's been a year and not a day goes by that there isn't something that I want to share with you. Growing up, all I needed was you three. Everyone else was a bonus and when you were taken from me, I realized just how lucky I was. This will never get any easier, but I want you to know that I love you. I also want to thank you for helping build a family that I could turn to. Without being able to come home to them, well, I can't imagine how difficult my life would be. I love you. I love you. I love you."

Everyone is dabbing their eyes, even Dad, as Emma kneels on the ground. Her cheeks are red and streaked with tears, but her eyes blaze with determination. She doubts her strength but for everyone looking at her in this moment, it shines from her.

Emma continues to speak softly, and out of respect I lead

everyone except Alex to the gazebo. Standing in the entrance, I watch him help her up and walk with her towards us.

"That should be me," I say as Lia steps up beside me to watch them. Emma smiles at something Alex said. "At least when she looks at me, it's not a hardened expression void of emotion anymore." Lia squeezes my arm comfortingly, I'm thankful that she doesn't say something to remind me it's my fault I'm not out there.

"We should get the slideshow ready." Nodding, I follow her. Lia loads the slide show and hands me the remote as Emma and Alex enter the gazebo. I'm pretty sure I see Emma say "wow" as she looks around. Alex guides her to the table we have set up in the center and she sits down.

"Emma, we know that this is not easy for you and wanted to show our support. They say a picture is worth a thousand words." Heart pounding as I speak, her brilliant green eyes fixed on mine, I push play, my eyes glued to her as she looks to the screen.

Her hand is shaking as she lifts it to her mouth, watching the pictures and words on the screen. Alex did an impeccable job melding three people's lifetimes into a five-minute slideshow.

As the last picture fades Ryan stands up and gives her a hug. Speaking lowly in her ear as she wipes tears from her cheeks. She giggles and I'm glad for my big brother and his ability to make people find joy in even the toughest of times.

"Before we eat, we wanted to share some of our favorite memories with you. This is a celebration of life and let's celebrate them." Ryan's deep voice booms over the room. He starts with a story of how William worked with him tirelessly teaching him how to be a farrier. The art of trimming a horse's hoof correctly.

One by one, each of us tells our story until it's my turn.

Taking a deep breath, I stand and look at Emma. "When you were seven, I sat down with your mom and dad to have a serious conversation. You had hurt yourself and even though it wasn't my fault, my eight-year-old brain felt bad for not protecting you. I told them that I was going to marry you one day and that I would always do my best not to let you hurt.

"Back then I thought I could prevent the hurts and your parents just smiled and listened as I proclaimed how much I loved you. I haven't kept up with my promises to them, but what sticks out to me the most is when your mom looked at me and said that love isn't preventing the hurt, it's being there during the hurt. Those words have always stuck with me. It may not always seem like it, but I'm here for you when you're hurting, when you're angry or sad. When you're happy or excited. No matter what, I'm here." Lia coughs slightly and I realize I am rambling so I sit down quickly while Mom demands everyone eat.

Emma gets up from the table, her eyes on me, before grabbing a plate and dishing up some food. After she has a full plate, she slips out the door.

CHAPTER TWENTY-FOUR

Emma

Needing a breather, I step outside and sit on the bench under a tall elm tree. Dane's words in my head as I eat a delectable slice of cheese cake. He has loved me since he was eight? Why didn't he tell me?

After everyone had gone inside, Alex had told me Dane arranged the entire day with the help of his family. He has been watching me all afternoon and any doubts I had, even the shame and embarrassment, has diminished. Mom would have said that to him, and it was fitting that was the memory he told. It's something I need to remember. Love, friendship, family. It doesn't matter, you are there for the hurts. We've hit some bumps along the way, that wisdom easily forgotten.

"Emma . . ." Dane sits next to me and takes my empty plate. Huh. I didn't even realize I had eaten everything. "I was going to wait until we were home. Until you were ready to talk to me. I can't anymore. I swear nothing happened. I—"

Reaching out my hand, I lace my fingers with his, interrupting him. "I know. In the moment, I didn't have the capacity to deal with what I saw and the fear I felt." He traces circles over my hand, and the feeling of love and comfort I always get from him fills me. "Thank you for today."

"Anything. I will always do anything for you."

"Your words, that is so my mom. I can't believe you remembered that all this time." He smiles at me, his dimples creeping out.

"They stuck with me. I know I've forgotten them sometimes, I haven't always been there, but I have one promise that I can keep. I won't forget them again. I know now I can't keep hurt from you, I can't protect you from everything not even myself, but what I can do is always be there." Dane lifts his hand to my face and I lean into it. The rough skin of his palm scratching me, but I barely notice.

"We've both forgotten to do that. What we have is worth it. I'm not going to run away from my fears anymore, I'm going to face them head on. With you by my side." Sliding my hands around his head and into his hair, I pull him in and kiss him. As our lips touch, the pieces of my heart that had yet to be repaired fall back into place.

With a moan, I deepen the kiss, forgetting where we are or that people will notice us missing and enjoy the feeling of Dane's lips on mine. We've spent time together and time apart, yet from the moment I walked, err fell, back into Dane's life my heart knew what it needed. In that moment, it started a journey that I needed to go through and still need to go through. Yet as he pulls away and smiles at me with that mischievous and promising smirk, I know I'm finally whole again.

EPILOGUE
TWO MONTHS LATER

Dane

Collapsing onto the bed, sweaty and satiated, I smirk proudly at Emma. "I think we've found your favorite." Her arm is flung out to the side as she regains her breath, eyes twinkling humorously at me.

"Hmmm. Are you sure about that?" Her teasing voice sends shivers down my spine and if I didn't have something I needed to do, I would be wiping that smirk of her satisfied face.

"Well . . . If it's not we don't need to do that anymore . . ." I stroke her, feeling how wet she is, her body betraying her lie as she moans. "It's really too bad though, I had plans for tonight." Keeping my tone of disappointment, I pull my hand away and climb out of bed.

Emma pouts from my bed as I pull my jeans on. "What are you doing? I wasn't finished with you." She stands and stretches, never moving her eyes from mine, purposefully taunting me.

"Temptress. I want to stay in bed with you all day, clearly." She smirks as she sees my cock standing erect out of my jeans. "But we have something we need to do."

"I know, Arwen jumped out again." Emma starts to get dressed and despite myself, I can't help but look at the clock to see if we have a bit more time.

"Nope, I'm dressed now. You need to wait." Damn. Smiling as I pull her in for a kiss, she knows me too well already. I wouldn't have it any other way.

Arwen stands outside Emma's house and comes trotting over when she sees us. Automatically nuzzling Emma. The bond those two have formed has surpassed my dreams. Now that we are no longer in my bedroom, nerves are creeping up on me. I can feel the eyes of everyone watching from inside Emma's house. If I didn't need Alex's help no one would know, but of course now everyone does.

Emma is too busy cooing at Arwen to notice the delicate leather strap around her neck, and I'm starting to panic. Palms are sweating as I anxiously wait for the hand that is stroking the filly's neck to finally feel the supple leather.

The love I feel for this woman is overwhelming at times. We've both stood by each other through so many moments of happiness, anger, and sadness in the past two months. Emma continues her counseling sessions and more recently, I have attended with her.

She's finally starting to forgive herself for the part she feels she played in her parent's death, but at times I see the guilt flicker in her eyes. In those moments, I wrap her in my arms and just hold her.

Emma's fingers get closer to the leather around Arwen's

neck and I swallow nervously, the words I've been practicing running through my head.

She pauses as they brush the strap, heart pounding as she moves to Arwen's side and examines it more closely.

The gasp when she sees what is hanging there.

"What is thi—" She freezes as she turns and sees me on one knee.

"Emma, I have known I wanted to marry you since I was eight years old. Time, distance, misunderstandings . . . none of that diminished how deeply I love you. I want to be by your side for the rest of my life, grow old with you, make love to you, and build a family with you. You are my past, present, and future. Emma Hayle . . . will you do me the honor of becoming my wife?" None of those words are the ones I planned out in my head, but as her shocked green eyes glistened at me, I spoke from my heart.

Her silence sets my heart pounding until she collapses to her knees and is kissing me. "Yes!" One word. I thought when she said "I love you" was the happiest moment in my life, but hearing that one word has knocked it out of the park.

Kissing her deeply, we stand and I untie the leather, sliding the ring off the strap and onto her finger. Hugging her, bliss washes over me as I cherish this moment.

Our time is fleeting, made up of events varying in significance. Every second spent with Emma is significant and I intend to enjoy each and every moment, taking none for granted.

"I love you." Her eyes shine with happiness and I press my forehead to hers.

"I love you too."

The End

Alex and Lia's story, ***All About Hope***, is available now!

Sign up for my Newsletter: